"I've no int[ention]
of marrying...."

Caryn saw a smile cross Sharn's face as she said this. She added hastily, "It's so strange...." A haunting recollection of her wedding day drifted into her mind. "I'm married already...."

"Yes," Sharn murmured, "you're already married." The look in his eyes was strangely unsettling, and Caryn's mouth trembled slightly.

"You tend to forget." She found herself striving for composure. "Since it was never a real marriage, I suppose it's only natural."

He nodded, then frowned thoughtfully. "But there are times when you're forced to remember."

"Have you ever...wanted to marry?" Why was the question so difficult to voice, she wondered.

"I'm not in any hurry," Sharn replied. "I can make up my mind about marriage later." And he added, so softly that Caryn only just caught the words, "When I'm free."

ANNE HAMPSON

unwanted bride

Harlequin **Books**

TORONTO • LONDON • LOS ANGELES • AMSTERDAM
SYDNEY • HAMBURG • PARIS • STOCKHOLM • ATHENS • TOKYO

Harlequin Presents edition published July 1982
ISBN 0-373-10515-0

Original hardcover edition published in 1973
by Mills & Boon Limited

CHAPTER ONE

LIGHTNING zig-zagged time and time again through the great cumulo-nimbus cloud that had descended to blot out the sun. Thunder rolled ominously in the distance and within a few seconds the trees at the bottom of the garden became part of the deluge, transformed into mere distorted smudges within the semi-transparent curtain of rain.

Staring down from the window of her bedroom, Caryn frowned at the bleak spectacle and decided it suited her mood to perfection. Turning her head, she allowed her soft grey eyes to rest for a while on the photograph of Laurie that stood on the table by the bed.

'It can't be the end,' she whispered convulsively. 'He won't throw me over. We love each other . . .'

Why pretend – or hope for a miracle? Laurie had been most emphatic last night. With a distraught gesture Caryn thrust trembling fingers through her short dark hair, unable to accept that she had been thrown over for another girl. Surely Laurie would soon realize that it was her he really loved, and not the fair and elegant Grace Brownlow.

'Caryn!' The shrill complaining voice of her aunt broke into Caryn's misery and automatically she went towards the door. 'Where are you? It's long past tea-time!'

'I'm sorry, Aunt Beth.' Caryn sighed inwardly as she made the apology on entering the living-room a moment later. 'I'll put the kettle on right away.' She

5

went into the kitchen, which was behind the small grocery store owned by her aunt. Caryn had come to live with her aunt after the death of her father just over three years ago, and she helped in the shop.

'And don't give me any of that cake you made,' came the querulous voice from the living-room. 'It's like sawdust!'

Caryn's face paled with anger. The cake was perfectly all right, but Aunt Beth was in one of her fractious moods today. There had been no reason why she herself could not have put the kettle on, and prepared the tea, but Sunday was her day of rest, she maintained, and in consequence she refused to lift a hand in the house. Caryn's day off was Wednesday and for the past six months she had spent it with Laurie's mother, helping her with the chores, after which the two would sit over coffee and sandwiches and chat and later still they might go for a stroll in the park. At five-thirty Laurie would come in from work, and after the meal which the three ate together he and Caryn would go off to see a film, or merely walk hand-in-hand by the river, planning their future.

Their future. Not for another eighteen months could they marry, but Laurie had not seemed to mind. He loved her, he said, and so he could wait till the end of time for her.

And now he had found someone else.

'You've been crying,' Aunt Beth observed as she watched Caryn pouring the tea. 'I suppose it's for the same reason you were crying when you came in last night.'

'You don't understand. I love him—'

'You'd be better off remembering your marriage, my girl!' The woman's bosom heaved, manifesting her disgust. 'What's more, you should have been in church with me this morning, praying to the good Lord to forgive you for philandering when you have a husband!'

'I haven't got a husband, not really.'

'I seem to recall your being married right enough,' sniffed her aunt, accepting the tea her niece handed to her. 'In a registrar's office!' she added with grim emphasis. 'Not my idea of a place to be married – but you're married nevertheless, and don't you ever forget it! I told you at the start that Laurie wouldn't wait all that time.'

Caryn sat down at the table but made no attempt to eat anything. This nagging and criticism and harsh manner of speaking was becoming unendurable and recently Caryn had begun to wonder just how long she would be able to remain with her aunt. But there was something about the woman that incited pity in Caryn. She had never married, had spent her life building up her business and because she'd never had time for anything else she was now a lonely woman. And she had been even lonelier still before Caryn had come to live with her.

'If only I'd stopped to think, or refused to listen to advice, I'd never have married Sharn . . .' Caryn spoke involuntarily, to herself. Her aunt made no comment, merely sniffing and heaving her bosom in that maddening way, and Caryn allowed her thoughts to take a backward switch and for a few moments she re-lived that momentous period in her life. Brief it had been, but what unforeseen effects it was to have on her future.

It had all started when she was informed that she and a man named Sharn Cameron had jointly inherited a vast cattle station in the Outback of Australia. The owner had apparently known of their existence, while they had never known of his, so remote was the relationship. Having worked unceasingly to establish one of the largest cattle stations in Australia, this Mr. Drayford had – according to information received by the lawyer in England from the man's lawyers in Brisbane – been most anxious that the estate remained intact.

'He had extensive inquiries made and discovered he had two distant relatives.' The lawyer looked at Sharn and Caryn who, having met for the first time at the reading of the will, regarded each other with marked indifference as they sat there, in the musty office. 'As you both appeared to be equal in integrity and respectability he found himself in a quandary as to which one of you he would leave it to, his instinct being to leave it to the man, of course, but he felt that this was grossly unfair. He knew your ages as well as your backgrounds and he decided finally that rather than have the estate sold and the money divided he would make it a condition of inheritance that you married one another—'

'Married!' exclaimed Sharn, flashing a frowning glance in Caryn's direction. 'Then the whole thing's off.' He had stood up and would have left the office, but the lawyer waved a hand indicating that he should sit down again, which he did. He was a giant, a tough Australian who had inherited a sheep station from his father, but Caryn gathered that it was not of any great size compared to Sandy Creek, the ownership of which would make him one of the Outback's wealthiest graziers.

'You must remain married at least five years,' the

8

lawyer continued, absently perusing something on his desk before him. 'Mr. Drayford felt that this would ensure there was an heir.'

Caryn had blushed, while Sharn had looked at her with a decided element of distaste. Certainly he had no inclination to have an heir by her.

'Five years . . .' Sharn became thoughtful as he repeated this. He glanced at the lawyer after a time. 'That is the full extent of the condition? There's nothing else?' And when the lawyer shook his head, 'In that case there'd be nothing to prevent our having an annulment?'

'Nothing at all.'

Sharn frowned.

'It seems very remiss of the old man, don't you think? Didn't he consider this particular aspect of the case?'

'Apparently not.' The lawyer did however go on to say that although the couple could separate, the estate could not be sold up in order that they could share the money. In case of divorce Sharn was to retain the property and pay Caryn her share in cash. A sum mentioned was to be paid immediately after the divorce and the rest by instalments over a period of a further five years. This money would have to be earned, as Mr. Drayford had left no cash whatsoever to the two inheriting his cattle station.

'I couldn't think of marrying him,' Caryn had told her father. But he had always been of a mercenary nature and, fully expecting to share in his daughter's good fortune, he had allowed her no peace until she had agreed to the marriage. Sharn himself had several times called to see her father in private and after each visit Mr. Walsh assured Caryn that she had nothing to lose. 'Sharn's willing to give you a sum of money right away – an extra, or bonus, if you care to call it that. He says there'll be no complications whatsoever. You'll stay here while he takes possession of the ranch, after selling his sheep station. In five years' time you'll have an annulment and he'll then make over to you a substantial part of your share, as required by the terms of the will. Every year for the next five years you'll receive a further sum until he has bought you out completely. You'll be a very wealthy woman.'

The marriage was so distasteful, so very much a sham, that Caryn was actually crying when she came from the office on to the street crowded with Saturday shoppers. She and her father entered the waiting taxi and were driven home, Sharn already having gone off in his hired car. She had never set eyes on him since that moment.

Her wedding day ... She had always imagined a white flowing bridal gown, and bridesmaids, and a gay and never-to-be-forgotten wedding reception afterwards ... and of course, a honeymoon.

But her bridegroom, tall and handsome in a most austere kind of way, had left her immediately, having just sufficient time to catch the plane which would take him thousands of miles from the girl who was his wife.

Caryn's father had lived just long enough to squander the sum of money Sharn had sent to Caryn in consideration of her agreement to marry him, and then he had died of a heart attack, brought on, said Aunt Beth, by the fact of his having too much money for drink.

His death left Caryn without a home, as the house in

which they lived was only rented. When Aunt Beth offered Caryn a home she instantly accepted, blissfully unaware of what she was letting herself in for. Her aunt took ill within a few weeks and Caryn had not hesitated to give up her job in order to look after the business. And she had been helping her aunt ever since, working long hours for a mere pittance, and repeatedly deciding to leave and make her own way until, later, she would come into her money. But the old woman's loneliness cut deeply into Caryn's soft heart and she had never been able to carry out her intention of leaving her.

Six weeks after Laurie had thrown Caryn over her aunt died, and to Caryn's amazement she left her business and property to be divided between several charities. Once again Caryn found herself without a home, and this time, without a job either. In addition she was not by any means in the pink of condition, and so lethargic did she become that she visited the doctor with the intention of obtaining a tonic.

'Tonic?' he repeated, looking rather stern as he regarded her pale face and noted the nervous twisting of her hands. 'It's more than a tonic you need. What you want is a thorough rest, and a complete change of surroundings. You've been working too hard for a long while; I told your aunt this months ago when I dropped in to see her one day.' He set his mouth and was silent for a space. 'I never thought she'd be so callous as to leave her property away from you, not after the way you've helped her. I've never known such downright ingratitude.' Ignoring this, Caryn went on to point out that she could not take a rest, as she must get a job immediately in order to keep herself. 'And what about somewhere to live?' he asked, frowning heavily at her.

She shook her head helplessly.

'I shall have to look round,' she began, when he interrupted her. He knew of her marriage, naturally, because she had been forced to tell him of her change of name. He had known the family for a long while and in fact had brought Caryn into the world, almost twenty years ago. He had worked desperately but vainly to save her mother's life at that time. And so he felt he had the right to speak intimately to Caryn, especially now that she had no one here in England to whom she could turn.

'Your husband, Caryn – why don't you go to him?'

'That's impossible, doctor. I did tell you a little about it at the time, if you remember? It wasn't a proper marriage.'

Faintly he smiled at her way of putting it, but his voice was grave when presently he spoke.

'You own half of that property, Caryn, and I don't see why you can't go over there and make yourself comfortable until the time when you and your husband arrange the annulment.'

Your husband ... How strange it sounded. Caryn had been able to think of Laurie as her husband without any trouble at all— She cut her thoughts, for they were too painful by far. Only yesterday she had seen Laurie and Grace together, strolling arm-in-arm down by the river.

'I couldn't inflict myself upon him,' she said in firm decisive tones. 'We're complete strangers; he'd hate the idea of my intruding into his life.'

'You needn't intrude into his life,' the doctor pointed out reasonably. 'Those homesteads are almost always large and I'm quite sure this one will be no exception. You can have your own private apartments— No, dear, please don't interrupt me. You *are* joint owner of the property; it *is* your right to live there and partake of the ease and comfort which your inheritance has given to you. Your husband can't object – he won't, I feel sure, simply because he has you to thank that he has the place at all.'

'We both benefit. Neither has the other to thank.'

'Why should he have all the benefit at present – and you none? Why should you have to wait for five years?'

'That was the arrangement. You must remember that the annulment was our idea. Mr. Drayford hadn't thought of our – well, doing a wangle, as it were. He believed we'd live together, naturally.'

'He wasn't very far-seeing,' mused the doctor, for the moment diverted somewhat. 'Had I been making the will I'd have seen that every loophole was closed. His lawyers didn't go out of their way to advise – or warn – him.'

'I expect both they and Mr Drayford believed us to be honourable people, which we're not. Aunt Beth always maintained I'd be punished for marrying for money in the way I did. It was abusing the sacredness of marriage. . . .' Caryn allowed her voice to fade to silence as it began to dawn upon her that this aspect of the affair was irrelevant. 'To get back to the question of the tonic I came for—' She stopped as the doctor shook his head.

'Unless you want to have a breakdown you'd better be considering my proposition,' he recommended. 'You're in no fit state to tackle the problems of finding a home and a job. You say your aunt's left you nothing at all – not even a few sticks of furniture?'

'No, nothing.' For no particular reason Laurie intruded into her thoughts and before she could attempt to hold back the tears she felt them on her lashes. The swift sweeping of a hand across her face naturally brought the doctor's attention to it and he saw at once that she was affected by some emotion which had nothing to do with her physical health.

'What is it, Caryn?' he asked gently, and it needed only that to unleash her pent-up misery and the whole story was poured into the sympathetic ear of the doctor. 'I'm sorry,' she murmured huskily when at last she had told him everything. 'I shouldn't be taking up your time with my troubles.'

'I don't see why not – seeing that you haven't anyone else who can listen.' He paused a moment, frowning. 'This young man doesn't seem much of a loss, Caryn. Obviously he wasn't sincere; you do realize that?' He gave her a sidelong glance, supporting the question, and she nodded her head.

'It hurts all the same,' she said in a choked little voice. 'If I had Laurie now I'd not feel so dreadfully alone and lost.' She gave a sigh that was almost a sob. 'I feel a coward . . . as if I'm totally lacking in courage. I should be able to tackle a problem like this. After all, I'm not the only girl who's been left in such a situation.'

'You're no coward, Caryn. You're not well, that's why you're feeling so dejected and unable to cope. Go home and think about what I've said—'

'I can't inflict myself on a husband who doesn't want me,' she protested before he could finish what he intended saying. 'We're total strangers.'

'You say you have nothing at all – no home, no job,

14

no furniture. How do you expect to get yourself established?'

Caryn shook her head distractedly, wishing he had not brought her position so starkly before her mental vision.

'I have no idea, doctor, but I must. Perhaps I can get lodgings with an elderly couple who need some extra money. And I expect I can get some sort of a job without much difficulty. In eighteen months' time I shall be exceedingly well off, remember.'

'Perhaps so. And in the meantime? I've said, Caryn,' he continued softly, 'that you're in no fit state to tackle the job of settling yourself into a home and a job. Now, do as I say; go home and think about my very excellent advice. Write to your husband, telling him about your position – and I shall write to him too if you'd like me to. When you've explained I'm quite sure he'll raise no objection to your taking up residence in the home which, after all, does partly belong to you. It is half yours, Caryn. You appear to keep forgetting this fact. Your husband won't forget, though, I feel sure. But should he be unreasonable you have only to remind him of this joint ownership of the estate, to declare quite firmly that you intend enjoying the ease and comfort to which your inheritance entitles you.'

He talked more about this and Caryn made no attempt to interrupt. She was too weary to argue; she would listen – and then forget all that was being said.

But after having tried unsuccessfully to find anyone willing to let her a room or take her in as a boarder, and after a similar unfruitful search for a job that was in any way acceptable, she found her mind dwelling more and more on the kindly old doctor's advice. And when at length she was informed that she must leave the shop premises within a month she began quite seriously to contemplate taking that advice. The doctor was right when he implied that it was unfair for Sharn to be benefiting now, while she must wait for another year and a half. True, that had been the arrangement to which she herself had agreed, but since that time her circumstances had altered and she was now in almost desperate straits. Her health too was rapidly deteriorating and when, after enduring agonizing headaches brought on by nervous strain and anxiety she went once again to see the doctor, it was a stern and angry man she faced – not the kindly doctor to whom she had outpoured the story of her broken romance.

'No more nonsense!' he snapped after admonishing her for wasting all this time. 'I called at the shop, but it was closed, and you were out. I tried to phone you several times. You're far worse now than when you first saw me. In fact, I ought to send you off to be cared for in hospital. Shall I, Caryn – or are you prepared to be sensible and take the simple way out?'

'I'll write to Sharn,' she promised. 'But in the meantime, please give me something for these dreadful headaches.'

The doctor obliged, his manner softening now that she had given him her word that she would contact Sharn. This was showing a little sense, he told her, producing a smile even while a frown remained on his brow, caused by her pallor and the dark patches lying under her eyes.

'The complete change of environment and air, and the peace you'll find there, in the Outback, will soon put some colour back into your cheeks,' he declared as she was leaving. 'Remember what I've said, though, just take things easy. There's no need for you to do any work; you're just as much the boss as he is.'

This Caryn did not admit. Sharn was used to life on a sheep station and, therefore, it was reasonable to assume he was equally adept at running Sandy Creek even though it was much larger than the holding he had previously managed. She herself had no experience at all and she was more than willing to accept that Sharn was the real boss of the estate they had inherited. All she wanted was that he accept her, just for the waiting period. Once she came into her share she would leave, and never trouble him again.

She wrote and posted the letter and there seemed then to be a psychological reaction to the decision she had made for the thought of going over to Australia and occupying rooms in the homestead no longer troubled her. It seemed the obvious course to take, the easy way of dealing with the difficulties that beset her. As joint owner of the homestead she could not possibly feel herself to be an intruder. On the contrary, she would, no doubt, given time, become quite used to the idea that she was in fact the mistress there, while Sharn would remain the undisputed master. She might be able to help in the house, once she had regained her health and also thrown off her depression over the loss of Laurie. Yes, she might just be able to make herself useful, and if so nothing would please her more, since she had no wish to spend her time in complete idleness.

And so it was with growing optimism that she made a few necessary purchases, booked her passage, and attended to all the other details which leaving the country entailed. And while all this was going on she looked expectantly from the window each morning on hearing the postman's van stopping and starting along

17

the street. Would he pull up outside the shop? she asked herself a little breathlessly. But he drove by and when a fortnight had passed she began to feel something might not be quite right. She visited the doctor, merely to have someone with whom she could discuss the matter.

'I should be flying out in two days' time,' she told him, her pale features drawn and anxious. 'Should I wait?'

The doctor shook his head.

'Something's gone wrong in the post,' he declared. 'His reply is probably late in arriving. I shouldn't worry, Caryn. Just carry on with the arrangements you've made; everything will be all right when you get there.'

She nodded, though she still frowned.

'I told him in my letter what time I would be arriving at the railway station—I have a long train journey after leaving the plane,' she went on to explain. 'I asked that someone be there to meet me and take me to the homestead. I do hope I'm not left stranded.'

'I should send a cable,' he advised. 'Just state again the time of your arrival at the station. Your husband won't leave you stranded,' he assured her with an easy smile. 'He owes you a great deal, remember.' Caryn said nothing and the doctor went on to remind her that Sharn would never have come into so profitable an inheritance had she refused to co-operate in the wangle, as she chose to term it.

She nodded automatically in agreement, her mind still occupied by anxiety.

'I do hope his reply arrives before I leave, though,' she murmured, frowning. 'I'd feel much better if I was sure of a welcome.'

The doctor was silent, his lips pursed. Caryn had no difficulty in reading his thoughts. It didn't matter in the least whether or not Sharn were ready to welcome her, he was saying to himself. She, Caryn, was entitled to take up residence at the homestead and Sharn must agree to this whether it suited him or not. This, however, was not the way Caryn wanted it to be. She was fully sensible of the fact that Sharn – quite under-standably – must by now be regarding the property as his own, and all that was incumbent on him was to comply with the terms of the will and buy her out at the appointed time. Large sums of money were involved – especially large was the first payment – and Caryn fully appreciated that he must be having to work very hard in order to amass this initial payment, since half of it must come from his share of the profits. Thinking about it, Caryn made the sudden decision to make it clear to Sharn that she would not demand so large a sum if this in any way inconvenienced him. They had done a wangle over the inheritance, she would remind him, and they could do another over the repayments. So long as she had sufficient to establish herself in a decent home she would not mind in the least waiting for the rest of her money.

'I feel confident you can be sure of a welcome.' The doctor's voice broke into her musings at last and she glanced at him. 'If the man has an ounce of gratitude in him he'll go out of his way to make you comfortable.'

Again Caryn nodded, but not mechanically this time. She was trying to recall her husband's face and presently saw the lean bronzed features, but was unable to bring them into as clear focus as she would

19

have wished. For she would have been more confident could she see a hint of softness about the face, a shade of kindness in the very dark eyes. Yes, she did remember the eyes, as they had seemed to look indifferently through her even while she gained the impression that their owner saw far more than it would appear by his apparent lack of interest in the girl whom he hoped would become his wife. She remembered also that outthrust chin and stern line of the jaw; she knew his hair was dark brown and shining with health; she vividly recalled the way he spoke – with a slow drawl that seemed almost to denote laziness. The long brown hands, however, instantly gave the lie to this impression, for they were strong hands, toughened by hard toil.

The doctor was beginning to repeat what he had said, in an endeavour to bring her from her reverie, and she gave him a wry and faintly apologetic smile.

'Yes, I'm sure you're right, doctor,' she broke in, saving him the trouble of finishing. 'Sharn will be sure to extend me a welcome.'

These words were recalled when, on her arrival at the railway station, she saw only one young man who was there to meet another man of similar age. Caryn watched the two greet each other and stand talking for a few moments. Several other people got off the train and went towards cars which had been parked at the station. All these cars soon disappeared, leaving Caryn and the two young men, both of whom, carrying suitcases, had begun to walk towards a large overlanding car in which the first young man had arrived. A station official stared at Caryn, standing there, by her luggage, feeling decidedly lost and, in fact, rather fearful.

'Someone coming to meet you?' he inquired, walking towards her.

'I expected someone to meet me,' she faltered, aware that first one of the men stopped and turned, and then the other did likewise.

'Where are you for?' asked the official, and Caryn replied without hesitation. The man frowned and said,

'That's about eight hundred miles from here. There might have been trouble with the car.'

'I see . . .' Eight hundred miles. Caryn had given a start on hearing this and only just in time had stopped herself from asking the man if he were sure about this distance. What a way to ask someone to come! She should have looked at the map and made some calculations as to the distance before calmly informing Sharn she would be at the station. Yes, she could have discovered that Sandy Creek Station was so far away, since it was clearly marked on the map, so the solicitor had said at the time of the reading of the will. Caryn had not been interested at that period, having already decided she would never be setting foot on her property anyway. 'Is there any place where I can wait?'

'You're quite sure they're coming for you?'

Her slight hesitation was very noticeable; the two men spoke together, and then, putting down the suitcases, they also came towards her. She flushed with embarrassment at being the centre of interest, but managed to sound untroubled as she replied,

'I think someone is sure to come and meet me.'

'Excuse me . . .' The man who had driven the car smiled at Caryn as he intervened. 'Did I hear you say you were bound for Sandy Creek?'

'That's right,' she returned eagerly. 'Do you know of it?'

'Sharn Cameron's place? Of course. We live about

forty miles farther on, at Katamunda Downs.' He frowned as he paused in thought. 'He's expecting you?' he inquired strangely.

'Yes – er – I hope he is.'

'You're not quite sure?' The young man's eyes wandered over her slender figure before coming to rest on her flushed face.

'I sent him a letter informing him I was coming—' She broke off, feeling most awkward at having to explain to the young man. It had never occurred to her that she would find herself face to face with anyone other than the man who was her husband. He would come himself, she had decided, so that he could talk to her, perhaps to give her certain instructions. He would tell her whether or not his friends and neighbours were aware of his marriage, or whether he had preferred to keep it from them.

'When did you send the letter? I ask because I and my parents are very friendly with Sharn and he never mentioned anything about expecting a home help. You are a home help, I presume?' His smile reappeared and this time it was accompanied by a gleam of amusement in his eyes. 'A pommy seeking adventure out in the wild rangelands?'

Was there a hint of sarcasm and a patronizing note in his voice? Or was she imagining things?

'I'm not a home help,' she returned, injecting a tinge of hauteur into her voice in spite of the fact that she was hoping for some assistance from the man.

'I'm sorry. Some relation, then?'

After a small hesitation she returned non-committally,

'I'm a sort of relation, yes.'

Although a trifle piqued at her reticence the young

22

man was plainly troubled as he told her that Sharn was definitely not expecting her.

'He would have mentioned it to us if a visitor were coming,' he added. 'In any case, he isn't at home at present.'

'Not at home?'

'His mother's sister is ill in a Sydney hospital and Sharn took his mother there to be with her. They haven't returned because this aunt isn't expected to live and she asked them both to remain with her. Sharn was always a great favourite with his aunt, and busy though he is at the present time – what with mustering and branding and the rest – he agreed to stay with his aunt till the end.'

'You know this?' murmured Caryn, diverted.

'We do receive communications – out there in the wilds,' he returned, and Caryn's colour rose at the sarcastic edge to his voice which, this time, could not possibly be missed.

'How long has he been away?'

'About three weeks,' he replied after a moment of calculation.

'So that's why he didn't answer my letter.' Relief swept over her at the knowledge that Sharn had not received her letter. For she had begun to wonder if, deciding he did not want her at Sandy Creek, he had deliberately left her stranded at the station. But that would have been a callous act, and she had no reason for associating this kind of conduct with the man who, after all, was her husband.

The young man was looking rather puzzled.

'Surely the arrangements for your visit were made earlier than three weeks ago,' he said at last, an odd inflection in his voice.

'No,' she replied without thinking. 'I wrote only about three weeks ago. He must have left before it reached him.'

'You wrote—?' The man broke off, shaking his head. 'I don't think I understand? You didn't just write, telling him to expect you?'

'Well . . . yes, I did.'

'You mean – you didn't ask if it would be convenient?'

Caryn did not answer immediately. It was impossible to tell the man that she had every right to move in to Sandy Creek because it was just as much hers as it was Sharn's.

'I didn't think it would inconvenience him if I came,' she said lamely at last, after both young men had moved impatiently, probably to remind her that she was taking up their time. The station official had already gone away and was now sitting in a small office, his head bent over something which looked like a desk. Caryn could just see him through the window.

'I still don't understand,' said the man, but immediately added, 'However, if you'd care to come along with us you're very welcome.'

'You'll take me all the way?' Her gratitude shone in her eyes and a smile touched the young man's lips.

'Of course. I have to go within five miles of Sandy Creek.'

'Oh . . . you're very kind,' she breathed, almost sagging with relief. 'I'm most grateful to you.' She glanced at the second young man as she spoke and something in his expression made her add, 'You don't mind my coming with you?'

He shrugged, in such a way that it was quite plain that he would rather travel with the one companion.

This man, Caryn was later to learn, was his friend from England, come to stay at Katamunda Downs for a year.

'Certainly he doesn't mind.' The first young man spoke for his friend. 'And now, into the car with your luggage – but first, the introductions. I'm Richard and this is Gregory. Dick and Greg for short.' He looked inquiringly at her and she told him her name, wondering what his reaction would be were she to use her married name.

'Caryn Walsh – welcome to Australia. I hope you'll have a happy stay.'

'Thank you,' she smiled, but gave an anxious glance in the direction of Greg. He was lifting up one of her suitcases and said quietly,

'You do know that we'll have to camp?'

'Camp?' she blinked, and Dick, also holding one of her cases, turned his head.

'We have to make camp, owing to the long distance. You don't mind?'

'Aren't there any hotels where we can stay?'

He laughed.

'Not where we're going, Caryn. But you'll be all right, I assure you.' He laughed again on seeing her expression. 'There's safety in numbers, remember,' he added, and she went a trifle red.

'Do you usually camp?' she asked, playing for time so that she could visualize the scene. A tent? Or did they just get down on the ground? The two men ... and herself ... Automatically she shook her head, glancing around in a sort of frantic way, as if some solution to the problem might just be found, here on the deserted railway station.

'We have to,' came Dick's reply. And he added in a

soft and understanding tone, 'I know how you feel. We're total strangers to you, but I assure you you're perfectly safe. However, if you want to decline the offer it's all right.'

She bit her lip, her eyes fixed on his face. He seemed genuine enough, but to Caryn's practical way of thinking it was taking an unnecessary risk, going out there, on an eight-hundred-mile journey into the wilds of the tropical savannah country, with two men she had known for only five minutes or so.

'I – I don't know what to do.' She looked apologetically from one to the other, instinctively aware that Greg's impassive expression was adopted merely to hide his impatience.

'You've nothing to fear, Caryn,' Dick assured her with a faint smile. 'Sharn knows me well. We've been friends since he came to Sandy Creek three and a half years ago. You can trust me, but, as I've said, I do understand, and if you feel unsafe then you'd better not come.'

This mention of Sharn was the deciding factor and she made no further hesitation. The bags were stacked into the overlanding car and five minutes later Caryn was on her way to her new home.

CHAPTER TWO

DICK chatted as he drove, while Greg maintained what to Caryn's mind was a rather sulky silence. She might be wrong, of course. He could be very tired after a long journey, as she herself was. However, so great was her interest in the vast country, a small corner of which actually belonged to her, that she determinedly kept awake when, after about a hundred miles had been covered, she could quite happily have stretched herself out in the back seat and fallen asleep.

'It sounds quite fascinating,' she offered at length, when Dick had described what went on in the running of a large cattle station. 'Imagine the cattle being transported in trucks. I always imagined they walked to the abattoir.'

'Driven along by stockmen and drovers? Yes, they went like that at one time, but it was a long weary trek for the men. Also, the animals lost weight on the way, naturally. So now we have the cattle trucks.'

'Tell me about the house itself. I suppose, in Sharn's case, he has to have a housekeeper?'

'Housekeeper?' Dick's voice had a strange edge to it. 'His mother lives with him, and also—'

'His mother?' she broke in. 'She lives with Sharn?' Somehow, Caryn had imagined Sharn living alone apart from any servants that might be necessary. She had not even known he had a mother living until Dick had mentioned her earlier. What a delicate position she was in, not knowing a single detail about the man to whom she was married.

'You didn't know this?' Dick was asking strangely, and Caryn pulled herself together.

'It had slipped my memory. Sharn and I have been out of touch for some time.'

'I see,' in thoughtful tones before Dick lapsed into a silence lasting so long that she began to wonder if he were becoming suspicious of her. However, he spoke at last, telling her that Sharn's mother – who had been widowed a second time – came to Sandy Creek about two years ago, having been ill and unable to look after herself. Soon afterwards her daughter, Sandra, and her husband, came on a visit and decided to settle in the Outback. 'Fred's now the schoolmaster— Some of us have small schools for our employees' children,' he went on to explain. 'Sandra helps in the house but also takes a turn in the shop. She and another young wife look after the shop between them.' He drove slowly on, taking a bend with care. Caryn had given a slight start on hearing of this Sandra and Fred, but this time she held her tongue, hoping to glean further information from things said by Dick. 'There's a houseful, as a matter of fact.' Dick spoke thoughtfully, as if to himself. 'Still, I expect they'll find room for another. There are always rooms reserved for visitors and chance travellers who ask for a night's lodging.'

'I understood it was a very large house in which Sharn lives?'

'It is, but there are so many living in it. However, as I've said, they'll make room for another one.'

Her mouth went dry. How had she come to take it for granted that Sharn lived alone in the great homestead? She had visualized a couple of housemaids and a more elderly woman in charge. There would be numerous rooms from which she herself could choose her 'suite';

she was going to live in the greatest comfort and luxury, and be so far away from Sharn that he could not possibly be annoyed or inconvenienced by her presence. Now, it appeared that she would be living 'communal' except for having her own bedroom.

'Who lives there besides his mother and Sandra and her husband?' she inquired at length, and was told about Mary, who was lame.

'But you must know about her,' he added quickly. 'She's made her home with Sharn since she was quite young.'

'Mary . . . Er, yes. She's lived with him a long time.' Who on earth was Mary? And why should she have made her home with Sharn?

'She couldn't stand her stepfather, if you remember? And that's why her brother gave her a home. She was with him on the sheep station – long before they came to Sandy Creek.' His voice cut off abruptly, and Caryn gained the rather strange impression that he had no wish to continue talking about Mary.

'That's right.' So, up till now, there was a mother, two sisters and a brother-in-law living on the station.

Scared at the idea of meeting all these strangers, Caryn would readily have turned back were that at all possible. But this was by no means the entire list of residents at the homestead, as she was soon to discover when Dick began to tell her about George, the Chinese cook, Sam the rouseabout, and the two lubras who kept the house clean. These four lived in at Sandy Creek. Then there was the foreman stockrider, Vic, who at forty-eight was still a bachelor and who, unwilling to live in the single men's quarters, had also been provided with accommodation in the house.

'I think that's about all,' said Dick, then instantly

added, 'I have mentioned Harriet? No, I don't think I have. She came as a home help from England about six months ago — and a very glamorous home help she turned out to be, I can tell you! She was soon promoted from the kitchen to the parlour, as it were. Now she does precious little other than making herself pretty for the Boss and helping him with his accounts. She's good at office work, apparently, as Sharn often praises her efficiency.'

'I hadn't heard of this girl,' murmured Caryn, who, for some inexplicable reason, wanted to know more about her – much more.

'You wouldn't have, not if you've been out of touch with Sharn. As I've said, she came only about six months ago.'

'She sounds as if she's become an important member of the household.' It was Greg who spoke, breaking his long silence at last. 'Is there a romance in the air?'

'There could be. Sharn's definitely attracted – at least, we all believe he is, and I'm sure Harriet herself has hopes of becoming the first lady at Sandy Creek. It's understandable that he's attracted,' Dick went on after a slight pause, 'as you'll realize once you've met the girl. Fair as a lily, with eyes like blue stars and the figure of an angel!'

Surprisingly Greg laughed, and his dark head moved backwards as he did so. Caryn glanced at it, noting the attractive pageboy bob styling and the shining cleanliness of the hair. He was good-looking, too, and she decided he could be inordinately attractive were he not so sulky – or perhaps, she amended, since she had not had time to form a proper opinion of him, he was merely the quiet type who preferred listening to talking.

'Sends you all poetical, eh? Not fallen for her yourself, have you?' he asked, and a strange little silence followed.

'Not my type. I prefer someone a little more deep. Harriet would be delightful in bed but a dead loss in an emergency—' He stopped abruptly and turned his head. 'I say, I'm awfully sorry! I quite forgot we had a female with us!'

'That's all right,' she laughed. 'You've no need to apologize. Tell us some more about this Harriet. You say you wouldn't be surprised if Sharn married her?'

'Those weren't exactly my words,' he corrected. 'I said he was attracted to her, but marriage is a serious step and up till now Sharn's managed to avoid it, as you very well know.' He paused on slowing down to allow a flock of birds to get clear of the road without his hitting any of them, and Caryn used this brief interlude to smile to herself and muse on what reaction she would receive were she to tell Dick that she was Sharn's wife. Naturally she refrained, not blaming Sharn in the least for keeping his marriage secret. There was no necessity at all for his disclosing it – not when it was to be dissolved. 'I expect he'll decide to marry one day, though,' Dick went on as he increased his speed again. 'He's thirty-two, so he's probably thinking he'd better be doing something about producing an heir for Sandy Creek.'

'What's he like—?' Caryn broke off, having had no intention of asking a question like that.

'What's he like?' repeated Dick in some amazement. 'Don't you know what he's like?'

'It's such a long time . . . I mean,' she faltered, cursing herself for that stupid slip of the tongue, 'one tends to forget . . .'

To her profound relief she saw him nod his head.

'I expect you do,' he agreed. 'Well, Sharn's the tough leathery type like the rest of us who spend our time in the saddle from dawn to sundown. He's friendly but never expansive, and until the advent of the delectable Harriet he never bothered much with females— Oh, I say, Caryn, must I apologize again?'

'Of course not; you're only stating facts.'

'That's all I can tell you about him that you don't already know. Surely you haven't forgotten his shape and colouring?' he added with a light laugh.

'No, I clearly remember those.' It struck her that Dick was being extraordinarily tactful, since his curiosity must undoubtedly be aroused concerning her strange behaviour in coming out here without making absolutely sure she was expected.

He and Greg maintained a long silence and Caryn leant back and dozed for a while. When she opened her eyes she began taking a real interest in her surroundings, discovering, a little to her surprise, that although the landscape was flat and uninteresting, it appealed to her in some strange unfathomable way. She found beauty in the wide grasslands through which they were passing as they travelled in a north-westerly direction towards Capricorn, which they would cross on their way to the Northern Territory, where Sandy Creek Station was situated; she became absorbed in the strong colours – the bright red earth lit by sunlight, the varying greens of the vegetation, the brittle blue dome of the vast Australian sky.

A long while passed before Dick spoke again, and this only after twisting his head round to ascertain whether or not Caryn was awake.

'I hope I didn't give you the wrong impression of

Harriet, Caryn. She seems popular with Sandra and her husband, and with Sharn's mother.'

'No, you didn't give me a wrong impression.'

'I'm glad. It was with my remarking that I prefer someone with more depth to her character. Harriet always seems – to me, that is – to live on the surface, taking what's available at the moment and not troubling herself much about the serious things of life—' He broke off, and Caryn suspected that, could she see his face, she would discover that it portrayed annoyance with himself for speaking in this way. His next words more than confirmed her suspicions. 'I talk out of turn! I suppose that now I have given you the wrong impression about the girl?'

He had, but Caryn reserved judgment anyway. She never formed an opinion of anyone on what she heard from other people.

'I expect I shall decide what she's like once I've met her,' she responded at length. 'If Sharn likes her, and if she's popular, as you say, then there can't be very much wrong with her.'

Dick seemed satisfied that he had undone any damage he might have caused and for a few minutes he chatted to his friend, leaving Caryn to her own thoughts. She found herself absorbed by this girl Harriet whom, it appeared, Sharn liked very much indeed. Perhaps he did have ideas about making her his wife, once he was free. If this were the case then the girl might be in his confidence, having been told the reason why a marriage could not yet take place. This train of thought naturally led on to Laurie, who had vowed he could wait till the end of time for Caryn. But it was very plain that he had not really been in love with her; this fact Caryn faced, and accepted. And great though her hurt was — for she still cared deeply for him, and had he returned she would willingly have taken him back — she was practical enough to admit that a marriage between them most probably would not have succeeded. It would have been too one-sided, her own love being strong, while Laurie's was weak. No, it had all happened for the best — yet the pain remained just the same. It would remain for a long while, simply because, like any other girl who had gone through a similar experience, Caryn *would* keep dwelling on what might have been, had Laurie cared in the way he had always vowed he cared, swearing that he loved her to distraction.

One thing she was sure of, she told herself emphatically, no other man would ever throw her over for another girl. He would not be given the chance! She was finished with men altogether, finished because of what Laurie had done to her.

A deep sigh escaped her and she leant back, turning her head to find a resting-place. And within a few minutes she was fast asleep.

She awoke to see the sun's last dying rays spraying the acacia plains with deepest bronze, while the low hills away to the south-west were clothed in rich shades of purple, being, as they were, in the shadows cast by fleecy clouds.

'Ready for something to eat?' Only when Dick spoke did she realize that there was no longer any motion and she sat up guiltily.

'I should have helped,' she murmured, rubbing her eyes. 'There's a good smell!'

Dick had the car door open and she stepped down, helped by his extended hand under her elbow.

34

'Stewed steak and mash. Hope you like it?'

'I'm sure I shall,' she laughed. 'I could enjoy dry bread, I'm so hungry. How long have I been asleep?'

'Hours. We've covered about three hundred and fifty miles today.'

'You were driving fast.'

'For most of the time, yes. One has to here, where distances are so long.'

The two men had made camp close to a river valley; the stream was dry at present, but vegetation grew thickly along its banks.

'What kind of trees are they?' she asked as she sat down on the ground-sheet beside Greg.

'Red river gums,' answered Dick.

'Coolibahs – they're the same?'

'Some people call them coolibahs, yes. See the pretty marks along their trunks?'

Caryn nodded. She was now watching the last of the sunset, marvelling at the beauty of the wild deserted landscape. No sound other than that which they made themselves; no traffic or smoke, no scurrying mass of humanity. Just silence and stillness – and peace. She knew a strange sensation of excitement, as if some new and wonderful adventure was hers for the grasping.

After the meal she was given a bowl of water, and twenty minutes or so of privacy while the two men wandered off into a belt of trees. Caryn washed her face and hands and cleaned her teeth. She brushed her hair and was already in her sleeping-bag when the men returned.

'Good night,' said Dick quietly.

'Good night.' She paused a moment. 'Good night, Greg,' she added, and heard him say,

'Sleep well, Caryn,' and he slipped into his sleeping-bag and turned over, lying with his back to her.

The following day something went wrong with the car and it took the men over four hours to repair it. This meant another night out in the bush, since Dick was far too tired to continue driving far into the early hours of the morning. So it was midday on the third day when at last they arrived at Sandy Creek, instead of the evening of the second day, as Dick had announced when asked by Caryn how long the journey would take.

'That's it.' Dick pointed to the stately Regency mansion snugly nestling among the trees. Hills rose to the rear, while in the far distance mountains shone like metal in the brilliant rays of the sun.

'I wish Sharn were home.' The swiftly-spoken sentence came unbidden. Caryn was scared, really scared of meeting all these strangers, people in possession who had no idea of her existence; much less had they any idea that she would be arriving, intent on taking up residence for the next eighteen months. 'Have you any idea when he'll be back?'

'I shouldn't think he'll return while his aunt still lives. She's dangerously ill, as I've said, so even now the end might be close.' Dick had pulled up and Greg was already getting out of the car. He held open the door for Caryn who, with a rapidly-beating heart, alighted and stood looking across a wide flower-border at the beautiful two-storied house. A woman came from the side, staring at the car as she advanced towards it.

'Dick! What are you doing here? Is something wrong?'

He shook his head; the car door slammed as he came round from the driver's side.

'We've brought you a visitor. A relative of Sharn –

36

Caryn Walsh. Caryn, meet Harriet Watson.'

The two girls stared as they shook hands. Caryn murmured,

'How do you do?' but Harriet made no response. She wore an almost insolent air; her blue eyes flickered as far as Caryn's feet and returned to her face.

'I don't think I understand?' she murmured, transferring her glance to Dick. 'You went off to pick up your friend.'

He nodded, and explained as briefly as he could.

'It's unfortunate that Sharn's away,' he continued, while his friend fetched Caryn's luggage from the car. 'But I expect you'll all make Caryn comfortable.'

The girl was frowning, and shaking her head. She either chose to ignore what Dick had said or she had not been listening, for she repeated that she did not understand.

'I'm sure there's some mistake,' she went on to add. 'Sharn certainly wasn't expecting a visitor.'

'I've just told you the whole story as it was told to me by Caryn,' said Dick with slight impatience. 'I've brought Caryn here and it's up to you and the others to make her welcome.'

Harriet's frown deepened; she transferred her gaze from Dick to Caryn and said,

'You're a relative of Sharn – so you've told Dick?' The insolent manner and edge of arrogance and scepticism to the voice, the way the girl's eyes raked Caryn's travel-creased clothes, the complete lack of friendliness – all these combined to bring a glint of anger to Caryn's eye, and to give her trouble with her temper. It took a great deal of provocation to arouse that temper in the normal way, but Caryn was weary and wanted only to be shown a room which, she sincerely hoped, would have its private bathroom adjoining.

'I'm a sort of relative,' she began, rather shortly but in a controlled tone for all that, 'and—'

'Sort of, Miss Walsh?' rudely interrupted the other girl.

'Miss Watson,' said Caryn, looking straight into Harriet's eyes, 'will you kindly have someone show me to a bedroom?'

That the three standing there were stunned was more than evident. They gaped as if unable to believe their ears.

'Are you speaking to me, Miss Walsh?' Harriet spoke with a quietness matching Caryn's own; her elegant head was lifted high. Looking at her, Caryn was sorely tempted to inform the haughty creature that she was part owner of this vast station, just for the satisfaction of seeing her robbed of her authoritative manner. But naturally she kept a firm rein on her tongue, thinking of Sharn, and his established position here, as Boss of Sandy Creek Station. She would not for anything act in a way that would result in a lowering of his prestige. She had only to await his return and he himself would see that she was made comfortable, and that she was treated with respect.

'I've asked that I be shown to a room,' she said. 'I'm very tired and would like to take a bath.'

'We'll say good-bye,' interposed Dick, with rather more haste than was necessary. Clearly he wished to get away and leave the two girls to sort things out between themselves.

'Good-bye, Dick – Greg.' Caryn gave them each a smile. Dick responded; Greg looked as if his face would crack if he did likewise. His dislike of Caryn was as inexplicable as it was obvious. 'And thank you again,

38

Dick, for being so kind as to bring me all this way.'

'No trouble at all. We'll be seeing each other again before very long, I expect.'

Caryn and Harriet watched the huge overlanding car slide off the concrete and disappear along an avenue of picturesque casuarina trees.

Caryn felt lost, and dreadfully alone and for a moment she wondered how she came to be here, in this vast strange land, thousands of miles from anyone she knew. All at once her decision to come seemed absurd in the extreme; it was an irresponsible and thoughtless one, and most certainly she would undo it if she could. However, she was here, and there were other people besides this Harriet – who acted as if *she* owned the place herself! These others surely could not be like her, Caryn decided, and asked once again to be taken inside and shown a bedroom. She would then meet Sandra and Fred, and Mary, who was lame.

'I'm afraid we haven't a spare bedroom.' Curt words and spoken with marked indifference. The glint returned to Caryn's eyes.

'Do you expect me to turn around and go back to the railway station?' she asked, and Harriet went red.

'I don't know where to put you,' she began, when Caryn interrupted her.

'*You* don't know where to put me? Am I to understand that you are in charge of this establishment?' Caryn saw at once that something in her tone and manner affected the girl and when she spoke again the arrogance had vanished from her voice.

'I happened to be here when you arrived,' she pointed out. 'I was quite naturally taken aback, not having been told by Sharn that you would be paying this visit.'

39

Caryn allowed this to pass without comment. Harriet had obviously forgotten part of the story she had been told by Dick, the part which revealed that Sharn himself had never known of the forthcoming visit.

'I asked that I be shown a bedroom, Miss Watson.'

The girl spread her hands.

'We haven't—'

'Perhaps I can speak to one of Sharn's sisters?' And without waiting for an answer Caryn stepped to one side of the girl and walked up the wide steps to the front door of the house. She had just raised the knocker and let it drop when a middle-aged man came from somewhere in the shrubbery that ran alongside the lawn. 'Will you carry my suitcases in, please?' she said and, after a swift glance from her to Harriet, he picked two of them up and mounted the steps.

The door was opened by one of the lubras; Caryn went past her into the hall, followed by the man. She told him to leave the suitcases in the hall and go and fetch the others. Without hesitation he obeyed, while Harriet, red-faced with anger at the treatment she was receiving, brushed past Caryn and disappeared through a wide, high doorway. Voices were heard, then a small silence.

'I'll go and see what it's all about!'

The next moment a tall rather plump woman came from the room, looked Caryn up and down, and then said,

'Perhaps you will explain how you come to be here, Miss – Miss—?'

'Walsh.' Caryn suddenly felt quite unable to cope. Harriet she had dealt with, but it had been a strain. Her head ached abominably and the lethargy she had known at home was upon her again. She would have given anything to be able to get into a bed and go to sleep. 'Miss Watson knows the story; she'll enlighten you. Meanwhile, would you let me take a rest?'

'Do you expect me to allow a strange woman to come into our house and take possession of a bedroom? – just like that, without so much as an explanation as to how she happens to be here?' The woman's dark eyes raked Caryn with as much insolence as those of Harriet. 'I'm afraid you'll have to account for this intrusion. Harriet says you maintain you're a relative of my brother. Well, you're no relative of mine, so I fail to see how you can be a relative of his.'

A long silence followed. Had she not been feeling so utterly dispirited and tired Caryn could have found something amusing in this last phrase spoken by the woman who, all unknowing, was in fact her sister-in-law. And what a sister-in-law! Thank heaven hers was not a normal marriage! If the others were like Sandra then they were the kind of in-laws one always aimed to avoid.

'I think,' suggested Caryn at last, 'that you'll have to put me up, until Sharn arrives back home. Then he himself will sort the matter out.' Sandra was frowning thoughtfully and Caryn added, 'I can scarcely go back; and as there isn't an hotel where I might stay, then you've no option other than to give me a bed.'

Sandra's frown deepened; colour mounted her cheeks, angry colour.

'I'll let you have an empty bungalow which happens to be available. You must manage with that until I can get in touch with my brother—' She broke off as the front door swung inwards behind Caryn, who turned automatically. Sharn stood there, framed in the wide

41

doorway, a giant with a sun-bitten face and a puzzled expression in his eyes.

'Sharn!' Caryn sagged with relief and moved a step closer to him. 'Oh, I'm *so* glad you're here!'

'Caryn . . .?' The one word came slowly and his eyes flickered. He scarcely remembered what his wife looked like.

'So you know this woman?' sharply from Sandra, who without waiting for his answer went on to say, 'She maintains she's a relative of ours, and demands to be given accommodation.'

A silence followed while Caryn and Sharn stared at one another. She noticed how tired he looked – and how puzzled.

'A relative?' he murmured.

'I said I was a sort of relative,' she returned, throwing him a glance of reassurance. Caryn did not wish him to be troubled that she might reveal the fact that she was his wife. He inclined his head ever so slightly, thanking her. Then he glanced at the four suitcases standing neatly against the wall.

'Come into my own little sitting-room, Caryn,' he invited. 'We can talk in private there.'

'In private?' snapped his sister. 'What is all this about? This girl's no relative of ours!'

The dark eyes moved, then settled on his sister's face, fire smouldering in their depths.

'I've said we shall talk in private, Sandra. Meanwhile, have a room made ready for Caryn.'

'Caryn . . .' Sandra hadn't shown much reaction the first time he mentioned the name, but now she appeared to be repeating it silently to herself. 'There seems to be some mystery,' she began, when her brother interrupted her, repeating his request that a room

42

should be made ready for their visitor. And even as he spoke he had a hand under Caryn's elbow and was guiding her along the hall towards a door on the left. 'Aunt Jessica?' Sandra spoke swiftly, as if she would bring him back so that she might even now force a full explanation from him. 'Is she . . . dead?'

'She is,' with a distinct catch in his voice which surprised Caryn, because his whole appearance was so tough, and because there was a certain hardness about his features and in those very dark brown eyes. 'Mother and Aunt Dorothy and her husband are seeing to the funeral. There was no need for me to stay. Aunt Dorothy and Uncle Joseph are bringing Mother home later. Meanwhile, she wants to stay with them for a month or two.' He had stopped and turned, but as the last word left his lips he moved on again and on entering the sitting-room he closed the door, then stood with his back to it, staring intently at his wife.

'Sit down,' he invited after a while. 'And let me hear what it's all about.'

She felt shy and tongue-tied, wondering why she had not, at the time of the marriage, noticed this man's air of superiority, his self-assurance and commanding personality. She felt small and insignificant in his presense; the excuse she had to offer for coming here seemed totally inadequate. Only now did it occur to her that she could have acted very differently, asking for some money instead of assuming there was only one path to follow. It was partly the doctor's fault, she thought, since coming out here was his idea in the first place. She needed a change of surroundings and a complete rest, he had said. Had she written to Sharn, explaining her circumstances, then of a certainty he would have advanced her money, and with this she

43

could have had the rest and the change of surroundings; she could have taken herself on a long holiday.

Sharn gave a slight cough; she was reminded of his request for an explanation and she began to speak, rather haltingly at first but gradually gaining confidence as he listened with interest but without interruption.

'And that's the whole,' she ended, looking anxiously into his face. 'The doctor's advice was that I come out here for eighteen months, and I've taken that advice.' Her eyes, still anxious, remained on his face, which was an unreadable mask. He was not pleased, though. This fact was somehow impressed on her mind. 'I – I hope you won't be too inconvenienced by my being here?'

He spoke at last, taking possession of a window seat and automatically stretching out his long legs in front of him.

'Did it never occur to you to ask me for some of your money?'

'Not at the time,' she apologized. 'Just now I thought of it . . .'

'A little late,' he observed in a distinctly dry tone. 'However, it's not too late. I'll make arrangements for you to receive an allowance each month. And of course you shall have the money for your fare back to England. I'm sorry about your misfortunes, Caryn, but from the financial aspect you have no worries at all; you're a wealthy young lady. You knew this and I'm amazed that your doctor – who appears to have been deeply concerned about you – didn't remind you of it.' A small pause and then, 'You did confide the whole in him, I presume?'

She nodded.

44

'He knows I have – er – great expectations, as it were.' Faintly she smiled, but the severity of her companion's face remained unrelaxed and her smile faded almost at once.

'You'll be willing to fall in with my suggestion?' he queried, and after a mere moment of hesitation she said yes she would be quite willing to accept an allowance. Not that she wouldn't have liked to stay in Australia for a while, because she felt instinctively that the peace and tranquillity of the Outback would appeal to her in a high degree. It would be wonderful to relax completely, to go for long walks, to have the pleasure of the breathtakingly beautiful sunsets . . . Caryn allowed her musings to fade. For on the debit side was the family of her husband. True, she had met only Sandra, but somehow, Caryn sensed that the others would be no better. Then there was Harriet, whose arrogance would assuredly have become so galling to Caryn that an explosion would have been inevitable. She was ready to be accommodating, but only where Sharn was concerned. Caryn felt she owed him this and not for a moment would she embarrass him by letting it be known that he was not the sole owner of the cattle station. But should Harriet continue to adopt the high-handed manner, acting as if she were mistress here already, and treating Caryn with the condescension she had already displayed, then retaliation on Caryn's part must undoubtedly ensue. And as this would cause Sharn the embarrassment which she wished to avoid, Caryn had no second thoughts about her decision to fall in with her husband's plan.

'And now,' he said when the allowance had been further discussed between them, 'we've to satisfy the family's curiosity. As you've quite obviously gathered,

I kept the marriage secret. There was no need to reveal it, since it was to be merely temporary. I think we must tell them that we met when I was over in England three and a half years ago, and that, on talking together, we discovered we were very distantly related – owing to your grandfather having married a distant cousin of mine.' For the first time she saw the hint of a smile appear on those firm hard lips. 'It's rather fortunate that we are related – though just how we don't know – because you're a young woman who hates deceit – you did at the time of the marriage, I seem to remember—'

'I did hate it! I'd never have agreed to marry you had it not been for Father.'

'I was fully aware of the pressure, Caryn. Yet we haven't harmed anyone. As you know, the property was to go to the State if we failed to comply with the terms of the will.' She was nodding, though absently. Deceit was deceit no matter what colour it was painted, and Caryn was ever conscious that she and Sharn had done wrong. Had they agreed to enter into a normal marriage, producing the heir which old Mr Drayford hoped would eventually inherit what he had spent his whole life building up then – to Caryn's mind – no crime would have been committed. 'Getting back to what I was saying: we must indulge in a little more deceit in order to satisfy my family. You are in agreement about this?'

'I have to agree, since there's no other way. When I said we were related I had in fact forgotten the slight relationship which occurs through Mr Drayford. I was so flustered – finding myself stranded on the station with only complete strangers to listen to my troubles – that I said I was a relation of yours. Dick had to be given some explanation, as you can understand?'

'Of course. Don't look so troubled, child.'

'He thought at first that I was a home help – come out here for adventure.'

Sharn laughed.

'And I expect your hackles were instantly up? I admire your control. Had I been in your position I'd have had the greatest difficulty in holding back the information that I was joint owner of Sandy Creek Station.'

'I wouldn't make things awkward for you by revealing that,' she said with a smile.

'Thank you Caryn.' He looked at her long and hard. 'You're a nice girl,' was his unexpected comment, and for no reason at all she was plunged into confusion.

'It's – very kind of you to say so,' she murmured, flushing slightly and looking down at her hands.

'You're tired,' he observed. 'I expect your room is ready by now.'

'Thank you.' She managed to glance up, hoping her heightened colour was not too much in evidence. 'Will there be a bathroom? We've camped out for two nights.'

He nodded.

'I'm sure my sister will have given you a room with a bath.'

But the room to which Caryn was presently shown by Daphne, one of the lubras, was small and scantily furnished, with a single bed and a small wash basin in one corner. The window was high and tiny; it looked out on to the wooded enclosure at the rear of the house. Caryn stood in the doorway, biting her lip, and feeling absurdly close to tears. But presently she shrugged and asked that her luggage be brought up. It was only for a short while – just until Sharn could arrange her flight back to England – so what did it matter if she was not given the room she had expected? Room . . . A suite, she had imagined occupying. But then she had visualized only Sharn and the servants. Certainly the idea of a large number of people living at the homestead had never for a moment entered into her scheme of things on making her decision to come out to Sandy Creek.

CHAPTER THREE

'How long shall I stay?' Caryn was asking the question later in the day, after having taken lunch with several of the people mentioned by Dick. It had not been a pleasant meal, despite the friendliness of Sharn, who went out of his way to make his wife feel comfortable. But the animosity of the other members of the family was apparent, and that of Harriet glaringly so. Why they should dislike her Caryn could not fathom and she began to wonder if this resentment of intrusion was a normal trait of the Australian people as a whole. Yet Sharn was amicable enough and, to Caryn's relief, so was Mary. Caryn felt she had an ally in the girl who, at twenty, had given up all hope of marriage, because she was lame, having been born with one leg shorter than the other. Mary was sweet-natured, though, and this showed in the softness of her deep blue eyes and the fullness of her mouth. She possessed a figure as slender and attractive as that of Caryn and her hair was long and fair and fell to her shoulders in deep natural waves.

'It'll have to be about a week, as I can't spare the time to take you to the railway station. You don't mind?'

'N-no,' she said after a slight hesitation. 'It won't be longer than a week?' she added unthinkingly, and her husband tilted his head in a gesture of interrogation.

'You'd rather go at once?' and before she could reply, 'You intended staying for eighteen months, you said?'

'I didn't know then that there'd be so many people here.' She and Sharn were on the verandah and she was suddenly diverted by the laughter of a jacko somewhere in the distance.

Sharn was apparently puzzled by her remark.

'You expected me to be living alone?' he queried, an odd inflection in his voice.

'That was the impression I'd somehow formed,' she confessed. 'I imagined your having servants here, of course, but that's all.' A small deprecating laugh escaped her. 'We never exchanged any confidences, if you remember? – and so I'd no idea you had any relations.'

He shrugged, reminding her that his mother also lived with him.

'She was ill two years ago and couldn't look after herself. Sandra was living near, but she went out to work, so I agreed for Mother to come here. Then Sandra wanted to come and live here to be near her.' He paused a moment and Caryn had the impression that he was frowning inwardly. 'I agreed. Fred her husband's a schoolteacher, and we were shortly to be requiring a replacement for our young schoolmistress who was getting married. It seemed to fit in very well. Mary's lived with me a long time – since she was eleven years old. You see, Mother married a second time and neither I nor Mary could get on with the man. I already had the sheep station and Mary asked to come, and live with me. Naturally I agreed, as I had no wish that the child should be unhappy.'

'Is your mother a widow now?'

'Yes; her husband died four years ago.'

A moment's silence followed. Caryn wanted to ask more questions, but feared her husband would not care to go more deeply into matters which, eighteen months hence, could be of no interest to her. She supposed he considered they weren't of any interest to her now, but for some inexplicable reason she was interested – very much so. However, she refrained from exhibiting her curiosity and instead talked about the journey, telling him a little more about her fear at the railway station and her relief on being offered a lift from Dick.

'He's a reliable sort,' Sharn put in when she paused a moment. 'He wouldn't have left you stranded.'

'I was afraid, just at first, of going with them – two strange men, especially when they said we'd be camping along the way.'

'You'd nothing to fear. Dick and his parents are very good friends of mine.'

Automatically Caryn glanced around her. Red and white bungalows surrounded by neat gardens stood some distance from the homestead, which was situated not far from a river; not far from the bungalows was another block which, Caryn surmised, comprised the living quarters of the stockmen who had no wives and families. Closer to the house, but still some good distance from it, were other buildings – stores for food and clothing and other necessities which were purchased in bulk from the cities and sold in the station shop. There were stockyards for mustering and branding, there were several garages; sheds for saddles and harness; buildings for implements and vehicles. There was a large barn with a verandah running all around it. Dick had mentioned shed dances held in large barns, so Caryn concluded that this one was sometimes similarly used.

'You're very interested.' Sharn's low Australian drawl cut gently into her thoughts and she told him at once that she was visualizing a shed dance, with the lights and the music and laughter.

'How do you get enough people?' she then asked, once again glancing around as if to illustrate the vast emptiness extending as far as the eye could see in all directions. All that broke it was the outline of cattle on a distant rise, with a lonely horseman moving about in their midst. 'The homestead reminds me of an outpost of civilization in an endless desert.'

A faint smile touched his lips.

'That's quite a good description. It's the operational base for the whole station which, as you know, extends over several thousand square miles.'

'As I know . . .' She looked across at him, noting the eyes narrowed against the sun. 'I really didn't take much notice of what the lawyer was saying.'

'You should have. You'll have to be businesslike once you come into possession of your money. It'll be a vast sum, Caryn.'

'It frightens me. I wish I had someone to look after it for me.' This came out unconsciously, a desire she had not meant to convey. Her thoughts were with Laurie, who could have looked after her money for her, had they become husband and wife. A terrible sense of aloneness swept over her and before she could even try to dismiss it tears had gathered in her eyes. She blinked rapidly, but a tear escaped on to her cheek. She brushed it away, but as Sharn's eyes were on her face it could not be missed.

'You're crying. Is something troubling you?'

She shook her head.

'No—n-no—' Her lip quivered and she looked apologetically at him. 'Don't take any notice. I'm just filled with self-pity. It'll pass.' She found a handkerchief and

52

blew her nose hard. The action brought a faint glimmer of amusement to his eyes, but his tones were serious and anxious when he asked if she would like to tell him what was wrong.

She began to shake her head again, and on her lips were the words, 'I wouldn't trouble you – a stranger,' when suddenly some force she could not control took over, reminding her that Sharn *was* her husband, no matter what the circumstances of their marriage. And in whom should she confide if not in her husband?

He listened, hearing all there was to hear about the romance which Caryn had been convinced would reach fulfilment in marriage.

'He wouldn't wait,' said Sharn musingly when she had stopped speaking. 'Did he know of your inheritance?'

'No, I didn't mention it. Somehow, it seemed – tainted.' Another apologetic glance before she continued, 'I know you don't think this way, but I can't shake off a feeling of guilt. I suppose that in time I shall forget the circumstances under which I inherited the money – or, I should say, half of all this—' She spread her hands, embracing the immediate surroundings which included the lovely mansion with its immaculate gardens and woodlands enclosing it on three sides.

'Do you think it would have been different, had he known of the wealth that was coming to you?'

'He found another girl, as I've said. I don't believe he'd have been influenced by the money. He wasn't like that at all.'

'You're very generous. For myself, I do believe he'd have been influenced by the money, and I'm glad you never mentioned it to him. You do realize, Caryn, that you've lost nothing, that you're better off without a

53

man like that?'

'My doctor said the same thing—' She broke off, her mouth quivering again. 'It's difficult to resign yourself to the fact that you've been thrown over. I expect a certain element of pride comes into it. No one likes their pride to be hurt.'

'You'll find someone else,' he told her with confidence, at the same time examining her features. She possessed a quiet kind of beauty and for the most part her eyes held a solemn expression, but when some deep sense of emotion took command whatever she happened to be feeling was manifested in her eyes. With pity and compassion came shadows, with humour came light – and with love came a radiance that transformed her whole appearance. Laurie had seen that radiance; Caryn truly believed that no other man would ever see it, not at any time in her life, since she had no desire whatsoever to cultivate even friendship with one of the opposite sex, much less enter into a deeper relationship. 'Yes, Caryn,' Sharn was saying, 'you'll find someone else.'

Looking across at him, she flushed at the compliment. But she shook her head.

'I don't want to find someone else,' she said in soft but emphasized tones.

'You still care for this Laurie?'

'Yes, I do.'

'What a waste,' he observed, almost to himself. 'He's not worth a single thought.'

'I'll recover, in time.'

'What are you going to do when you return to England?'

Her long hesitation was not lost on him. The truth was, she had no real idea. She could take a holiday, but

54

she did not relish taking one alone.

'I'll have a rest, first of all,' she said at last.

'You have to find a flat, or house?'

'That's right.'

'Will this doctor you speak of help you to get settled?'

'He might, if I ask him. He's extremely kind, and concerned about me.' She paused, waiting for some comment, but when none was forthcoming she continued, 'He wanted to write to you, telling you about my being off-colour and needing a change and rest, but I said it wasn't necessary. You see, I felt, at first, that you wouldn't want me to come here.'

Again he made no comment and Caryn was left to make her own guess as to whether or not she would be welcome, were she to insist on remaining at Sandy Creek for any length of time.

Sharn remained silent, his narrowed gaze fixed on the lone stockrider silhouetted against a brittle sky. As Caryn turned to follow the direction of his gaze another stockman appeared and the two seemed to converse.

'I was asking how you got enough people for a dance,' she murmured at length, turning towards her companion again. 'Do all your workmen come?'

He nodded.

'And neighbours. They come from far and wide, and stay the night if they've travelled extra long distances.'

She said, after a thoughtful silence,

'It's difficult to imagine the life here. The land ... it's so austere, so limitless.' She dwelt for a brief moment on the dramatic history of the 'Never-Never', and thought of the pioneers who had to battle against

55

dust storms and floods, against drought and raids by hostile Aborigines. 'It's a wonder anyone had the courage to come out and explore the heart of the continent in the first place.'

'Men will always accept a challenge. There's a sense of defeat in not being able to get at something. And, of course, we must take into account man's curiosity. The unknown naturally arouses it, and the adventurous can't resist exploring.'

'It must have been exciting.'

'I agree, though great danger existed side by side with the excitement. The pioneers were brave men.' He glanced towards the rise as he spoke; the two men had disappeared over it. 'I'm afraid you'll have to excuse me, Caryn,' he then said. 'I must get back to work.'

She nodded, but unconsciously bit her lip, wondering how she would spend her time.

'Is it all right if I go for a walk? I mean, there aren't any wild animals – or anything?'

'No animals that are likely to hurt you. Yes, take a walk by all means, but keep some of the buildings in sight. You don't require me to tell you how easy it is to get lost.'

'No, indeed! I won't go very far.'

The next moment she was alone, and feeling lost in a very different kind of way from what Sharn had meant.

The next four days passed with dragging slowness, Caryn wondering all the time how she managed to keep her temper. Harriet was quite openly cold and indifferent towards her, while Sandra just managed to be civil. When Sharn was present, which was only at mealtimes and perhaps for an hour or so in the evenings, she made an attempt to be friendly, affording Caryn an occasional smile when she thought her brother would notice. Caryn, no fool, knew full well the reason for this assumed amiability; it was there to render a complaint by Caryn impossible, for should she tell Sharn she was not being treated properly, he would naturally say at once that this sister was friendly enough towards her. After a while Harriet also extended the same friendliness when in Sharn's presence, and it was clear that the two women had discussed the situation and the result was this hypocrisy. Fred's attitude was the same, although he did appear to accept Caryn as a member of the household and at least he was never openly hostile.

Vic was charming with Caryn, a mutual liking having taken place immediately they were introduced to one another. He it was who took her on her first long walk, in the cool of the evening. He also rode with her on a couple of occasions when he had an hour to spare. They would go over to the cattle run where they would sit with the stockmen drinking billy tea and eating damper. Dick's friendliness also relieved the tension that seemed likely to build up with Caryn at this time. He came over with Greg in the Landrover and they all went to town where they lunched and strolled and purchased a few items from the store. Caryn bought souvenirs, tokens to remind her of the Outback, and of that corner of the continent which she had actually owned, just for a short while.

Sometimes she would become aware of a strange tugging sensation somewhere in her subconscious, but concentrate as she might nothing clear could be grasped – not until, on the evening of the fourth day

57

when, happening to be on the verandah alone, she heard the voice of Harriet coming from somewhere in the garden at the side of the house.

'I should have an extension here – a modern wing. And I'd get rid of most of the old furniture.'

'It's valuable. I don't think Sharn will let it go.'

'Do *you* like it, Sandra?'

'Not particularly. But it went with the house and Sharn's very fond of old things. Besides, he seems to have a soft spot for the old boy who left him this property, and feels he ought to leave everything as it is.'

'How ridiculous, being influenced by sentiment! We all have to accept change. Sharn's a millionaire – must be – and so he can afford to turn this place into a veritable palace.'

'I don't know about his being a millionaire. He never has much to spend, as you've probably noticed. I'm beginning to wonder what he intends doing with his money. He leaves it all in the bank – just as if he were saving it for something special.'

For me; to buy me out, thought Caryn.

'What could he be saving for? There's nothing he needs.' A small pause and then, 'If he asks me to marry him then I shall soon see that he enjoys his money. He works too hard, for one thing. He could sit back and let others do the work. Don't you agree?'

'All the wealthy graziers could sit back and leave the work to others, but they never do – not the private owners, that is. Many of these stations are now owned by syndicates who have managers to run the stations for them. But work's in a grazier's blood, and especially it's in Sharn's. He'll never give up working.'

'Well, I hope he doesn't work so hard when we're married—'

'You seem very sure of marrying my brother, Harriet. Has he given you some indication that his feelings go as deep as that?'

A small silence before Harriet spoke, but when she did speak her tones rang with confidence.

'I know he cares, Sandra, I can tell. Yes, I believe he'll ask me to marry him.'

'I hope you won't turn Fred and me out?'

'Of course not. Fred's far too valuable to us.'

To us . . . Uncontrolled fury surged within Caryn as she sat there, in the fading twilight, the welcome breeze fanning her cheeks. Us . . . The proprietorial manner which the girl adopted!

And it was at that particular moment that Caryn fully comprehended the signal that had been trying to make itself felt on several occasions since she came to Sandy Creek. She was not at all sure she wished to part with her inheritance!

Dazed by this revelation, she tried to form a picture of the situation should she decide not to sell out to Sharn.

'I must,' she told herself. 'I promised. That was the arrangement and I can't go back on it.' But Caryn found her mind reverting to the idea of retaining what was hers by rightful inheritance. Mr. Drayford had left half of everything to her, and no one had the power to take it from her – no, not even Sharn. True, she had agreed to all that was put before her by Sharn, who, she was sure, had acted in good faith, with no notion of being unfair in any way whatsoever.

'I can't go back on my word,' she whispered once again. 'It would be all wrong for me to do so.'

Was it a dog-in-the-manger attitude? she was asking herself the following day as she strolled away

59

from the homestead, taking a bush path she had found on her first ramble and with which she was now familiar. Had the idea of retaining her property stemmed from anger against Harriet, and in consequence a desire to make it impossible for her to become complete mistress of Sandy Creek? She would make additions, Harriet had said. She would also get rid of that beautiful Georgian furniture. Like Sharn Caryn loved old things; she had admired that furniture at first glance, even though at the time she was in a troubled state of mind, having been given so uncordial a reception. And as for an addition in the modern style – the girl must possess no aesthetic sense at all. The very thought of this addition, made by a girl who had no real connection with the property whatsoever, a girl of whom Mr Drayford had never even heard, was fuel to the fire of Caryn's anger and disgust. It strengthened her sense of possession, causing her to build up a barrier to the freedom of anyone who would make changes to the lovely homestead.

It was in her power to prevent Harriet from doing what she liked with the property. Yes, *in her power* ...

Walking along by herself, with no human or animal in sight, Caryn wondered if the peace and solitude would soothe her emotions, bringing them back from the heights to which they had soared, driven by indignation and anger and that steadily-rooting sense of possession. She should not allow herself to become so worked up, she admonished sternly. She had been off colour; her nerves had been playing her up. She had come out here for a rest and a change which, the doctor had assured her, would soon restore her to perfect health. And instead of taking advantage of what was available, she was working herself up into a frenzy over the property which until yesterday she had been more than willing to relinquish in payment for its value.

Gradually the tranquillity and isolation did have their effect and for the first time since she had overheard that conversation yesterday Caryn's mind was at peace. She would be sensible; she'd abide by her previous decision to let the matter of the property remain as it was.

When she had covered a mile or more she turned and began retracing her steps, and it was then that she spotted Sharn, riding the massive grey stallion on which she had seen him several times before. She stopped and stared at horse and rider, a pair ideally matched in strength and stamina and perfection of form. Yes, Caryn had very soon decided that Sharn possessed a physique that was perfect in every way. No unnecessary weight carried on that tall upright body, whose lean hardness was portrayed in every movement. A light spring in his step; a way of walking that made him seem as weightless as a breeze, and as swift. Complete self-assurance in those well-set shoulders, arrogance in the way he held his head. The brown hair, thick and wavy, growing low on his sun-bitten forehead, was hidden at present under a broad-brimmed sombrero. But last evening as he sat opposite to her at the crowded dinner-table, Caryn had been more than a little shocked on discovering that she would have liked to touch that shining hair, just to discover what its texture was like.

A swift smile broke over her pale face as she saw him lift a hand in salute to her. She waved a hand in response and remained standing where she was, aware of a faint breathlessness, and a sense of pleasure at having someone to talk to for a few moments.

He was riding towards her with a sort of supine grace, and on reaching her he swung from the saddle with the same ease of movement.

'Enjoying your walk?' he asked with a smile, looking down into her face, his eyes flickering with an odd expression as he noted the flush that had risen to her cheeks.

'Yes, thank you. It's lovely out here!'

'You sound most enthusiastic. Most people would find our countryside monotonous.'

She glanced about her, finding colour in everything she saw. The spinifex was golden in the sunshine, its silver-grey spears waving against a sky of pure sapphire flecked here and there with filmy white; a distant hillock stole colour from the sun's fierce rays – yellow and orange and ochre. The path on which she stood was red.

'I'm not finding it monotonous,' she said. 'On the contrary, I consider it most attractive.'

His straight brows rose in disbelief.

'Attractive? You do surprise me.'

She glanced around her again.

'You, Sharn – you must like it, surely?'

'Indeed, yes.' He spoke quickly and stared at the homestead, nestling among the trees. 'Luck is a strange thing; it can make or mar one's life.'

She nodded, following the direction of his gaze.

'We were extremely fortunate. Just to think – it came right out of the blue. I still don't know anything about our benefactor.'

'I've found out a little, from neighbours. He appears to have been a quiet, reticent man, though, keeping himself to himself. He lived for Sandy Creek, having built up the estate over a period of no less than fifty-two years.'

'The house was here at first, though – it must have been.'

'He inherited it, but there wasn't a great deal of land – at least, not in comparison to what there is now. He kept buying whenever he could. He made a fortune here.'

And Sharn would make a fortune too, she thought, once he had bought her out. Caryn's thoughts switched to Harriet, who hoped to marry him. She would be a very fortunate young woman, since she would have both a handsome and charming husband, and access to great wealth.

'What have you been doing?' she asked, rather hastily, as he stirred, glancing at the stallion as it cropped the grass at his feet. She wanted to keep Sharn with her for a while, just for someone to talk to.

'We're very busy with the mustering and branding at present,' he explained. 'We have also to bring in about a thousand calves for vaccinations and – and—' He stopped suddenly and she glanced up questioningly. He hesitated a moment longer and then, 'The bull calves have an operation,' was all he said, and she knew the word he had been going to utter at first had been 'castration'. This, Caryn had already learned from Vic, caused the bullocks to grow fat more easily.

'Do you use hot irons to brand them?' she wanted to know, and Sharn said yes, he was afraid they did, at which she shuddered visibly and expressed pity for the calves. 'How old are they when you do this?' she then inquired, and was told they were just a few weeks old.

'They come in with their mothers,' he added. 'If you're interested you can go over to one of the folds and watch what goes on.' He paused and added, 'The calves don't make too much fuss, I can assure you of that.'

She was frowning heavily.

'They must be dreadfully frightened – poor little things.'

'I admit they're frightened, but they're soon over it.'

She became thoughtful.

'Sharn . . . isn't it awful that we have to kill in order to live?'

He stared at her for a long moment, into her eyes, which were shadowed and troubled. Her mouth quivered slightly and she was unconsciously shaking her head. He seemed to be seeing her for the first time – and he appeared to be surprised at what he saw.

'People don't usually worry their heads about such things,' he said at last. 'Nature has ordained that this is the method we must adopt and there's nothing we can do about it.'

'Violence . . .' she whispered. 'So much violence in the world.'

'The killing is done in a humane manner.'

'The animals must know, though,' she returned with conviction.

'So you wouldn't like to live permanently on a cattle station?'

She made no immediate answer, but allowed her attention to stray to a flock of galahs soaring above the harsh flat bush, their attractive pink and grey colouring bringing a fleeting softness to the landscape.

'I don't know . . .' Why the hesitancy? Caryn asked herself. The wholesale slaughter of animals was another important factor on the debit side . . . and yet she could not honestly say she wouldn't like to live permanently on a cattle station.

64

'You don't know?' He seemed surprised, just as he had when she had spoken in praise of the countryside. 'There isn't much here in the way of entertainment — and there aren't the bright stores where you buy all those commodities that are quite unnecessary.' He was smiling in some amusement as the last words were uttered. Caryn said unthinkingly,

'I could never afford things that were unnecessary.'

'You will be able to, though,' he reminded her, and she added to his amusement by frowning. 'You're a strange girl, Caryn. I take it that you don't attach much importance to money?'

'Possessions can become an encumbrance.'

'True,' he agreed unexpectedly. 'Nevertheless, it adds to one's comfort if one owns a few of this world's goods.'

'Yes, I suppose you're right.' She was feeling depressed without quite knowing why. She said, looking up into his face, 'I shall be leaving soon, and I'll never see this place again.'

His head tilted in a gesture of puzzlement. Only now did she realize just how abruptly she had changed the subject, speaking her thoughts aloud.

'You can come again, on a visit, if you wish,' he told her, but she shook her head. She had no wish to return and find Harriet in possession of what had once belonged to her.

'I don't think I shall ever come back.'

He shrugged indifferently. It was most difficult to believe that he was her husband.

'Once you're free you'll be married in no time at all,' he prophesied. 'Then you'll have someone to take care of your money for you.'

'I shan't ever marry—' she broke off, then added with a thin smile, '—again. I don't want anything to do with men; I was too disillusioned with Laurie.'

Another shrug of those wide, erect shoulders.

'You'll get over that unfortunate business. It's new at present, but time erases all hurts and disappointments.'

This was true. Nevertheless, she could not imagine herself falling in love again – not the way she felt at the present time.

CHAPTER FOUR

To her surprise Sharn said he would walk back with her. The offer kindled a warmth within her which brought a glow to her cheeks and a swift smile to her lips. Sharn's eyes flickered strangely as he watched her; he seemed faintly amused, she thought, and wondered why.

Harriet was on the verandah; she turned her head as Sharn and Caryn reached the paddock, but the distance was too far for Caryn to note the expression that crossed the girl's face. But she did notice that Harriet sat up stiffly, and that she kept her head turned in the direction of the wide white gate by which Caryn and Sharn had stopped.

'Thank you, Sharn, for giving me so much of your time.' Caryn's eyes portrayed her gratitude and she received a smile from her companion. How inordinately attractive he was! She could not help staring as, having pushed his hat to the back of his head, he leant languidly against the gate, one hand pushed carelessly into his belt. His hair shone in the sunlight and she saw that although in the main it was dark brown, there were several other shades as well, especially at the front, where it waved so thickly and where the bleaching effect of the sun was clearly portrayed. His eyes were narrowed in that characteristic way which was now familiar; his expression was one of good humour, his whole manner quiet and calm and yet at the same time dignified.

'You mustn't thank me, Caryn,' he said, making

ready to mount his horse. 'I thoroughly enjoyed our little chat.'

'It was pleasant, having company.' She would have kept him longer still, but she knew it was hopeless to try. He was ready to be off and as he swung into the saddle she half-turned from him.

'You should get Sandra or Harriet to walk with you,' he suggested. 'Or Mary would do so. She doesn't walk far, but she quite enjoys short strolls.'

'I'll do that,' she responded, unwilling to say anything which would reveal the true position to him, reveal that the inexplicable animosity existing precluded any friendly advances or requests on her part – at least, where Harriet and Sandra were concerned.

He left her then, riding away towards a distant cattle run, where a great deal of activity seemed to be going on. The stockmen had been a long way that morning, Sharn had told her as she and he strolled back towards the homestead. They had been seeking the animals they wanted to bring into the folds. And as she looked now, shading her eyes from the brilliant sun, she could see many young calves being driven in, keeping close to their mothers.

At last she made her way towards the house, wishing she could enter without having to go anywhere near the girls she so disliked. However, the taking of an alternative path which would bring her to the back door would be far too pointed a snub and Caryn approached the girl from the road running alongside the front lawn. She nodded and would have passed on, to enter the house, but Harriet spoke, her tones sharp and her blue eyes glinting as they swept a glance over Caryn's slender figure.

'You've been out a long time. Where did you get to?'

68

'Where can one get to?' Caryn could not resist asking, and the girl's face coloured angrily.

'I just thought I'd better warn you about getting lost. We don't want everyone wasting time going out to search for you.'

Quietly Caryn said, making a move which brought her several steps closer to the girl,

'I've noticed on several occasions your use of the word "we". Have you some financial interest in Sandy Creek?' The sarcasm was so very evident that it amounted to rudeness, but such was Caryn's mood that good manners were allowed to go by the board.

'How dare you speak so insolently to me! I absolutely refuse to answer so impertinent a question!'

Caryn's eyes rested on the vacant chair opposite to the angry girl sitting there, on the vine-shaded verandah.

'Miss Watson,' she said taking possession of the chair, 'you seem to forget that I'm a guest here – a guest of Sharn. I believe he wouldn't be pleased were he to know how you've treated me, right from the moment of my arrival. Can you satisfy my curiosity and tell me the reason for your dislike?'

'I – you—!' The girl was plainly flustered; it was clear that she had not expected to be questioned regarding her attitude towards Caryn. 'This matter of your being a guest,' she began evasively, but Caryn interrupted her, repeating her question.

'I'm not aware I've shown any dislike,' Harriet then answered, and Caryn's pretty brows lifted a fraction.

'Are you implying that I've imagined it all?'

The girl's colour deepened. She replied blusteringly, 'Yes, I most certainly am!'

Contemptuously Caryn flicked her a glance, wondering greatly at her own self-confidence. It must be the awareness of her position as joint owner of this vast estate which produced it. But she had no intention of sitting here arguing for all that; the girl was in every way an object of disdain and Caryn's reaction to her words was to shrug her shoulders and say that it really did not matter, as she, Caryn, would not be troubling her much longer anyway. At which the blue eyes opened wide as Harriet said,

'What do you mean? Are you leaving shortly?'

Caryn bit her lip in vexation at having made the revelation. Had she realized that Sharn had not mentioned the fact of her leaving at the end of a week she most certainly would have kept the information to herself. But she had taken it for granted that Sharn had told everyone she would not be remaining more than a week. In fact, she had spent quite some time wondering what excuse he had made for the brevity of her visit. Why had he made no mention of her leaving? she wondered, then immediately decided that he hadn't considered the matter all that important. Harriet was waiting for a reply and, frowning, Caryn reluctantly informed her that she was leaving in a few days' time.

'So soon ...' The girl became thoughtful, her eyes wandering over the garden with its tropical flowers and shrubs and lovely eucalypts of many varieties. 'It's a short stay,' she murmured at length. 'It was hardly worth coming for — unless you're visiting other — er — relatives in our country?' She looked at Caryn, expecting some response, but she was disappointed. 'This matter of your being a guest,' she went on, reverting to what she had been about to say when Caryn interrupted her, 'neither Sandra nor I believed for one moment that you'd been invited, for Sharn would never have left without making arrangements for someone to meet you. In fact, we were sure that he would have made an effort to meet you himself, as Sharn is a stickler for correct procedure – in everything he does.' She paused a moment and then. 'A letter arrived by the mail plane and as it was from England I presume it was from you?' Caryn seethed at the idea of this girl examining her letter – or rather, the envelope in which it was contained. It was stupid, she knew, but her dislike of the girl was such that she felt she could have found fault with every single thing she did. Harriet was waiting, but Caryn merely sat there, tight-lipped, unable to speak for the anger that had welled up within her. 'A cable was later read to us over the air, but as we could not fully understand its meaning Sandra and I decided not to worry Sharn with it. He had enough to trouble him at that time.'

A long silence followed before Caryn spoke.

'You and Sandra appear to have taken a great deal upon yourselves. Wasn't Sharn vexed at not having the contents of my cable relayed to him?'

Another silence; when Harriet turned her head away to hide her expression Caryn knew instinctively that Sharn had in fact been annoyed at the action of the two women in keeping the contents of the cable from him.

'No,' said Harriet at last, 'he wasn't vexed. On the contrary, he said we had done the right thing.' The lie was allowed to pass, as Caryn had not the patience to comment on it. Harriet became thoughtful for a moment and then, as if she just had to ask the question, 'You weren't invited, were you, Miss Walsh?'

Caryn's grey eyes glinted. The impudence of the

girl to ask a question like that! How satisfying it would be to tell her that she, Caryn, had no need to be invited to Sandy Creek, simply because she owned half of everything – homestead, land, animals, buildings. Instead she said, her anger successfully under control,

'Sharn made me very welcome. That should answer your question.'

Faintly the girl smiled, without a trace of humour.

'A clever evasion, Miss Walsh, but it's very plain to me that you weren't invited. I believe you just came, because you'd got to know Sharn and – er – come to like him . . .?'

Colour leapt to Caryn's cheeks.

'What exactly do you mean by that?'

'Sharn's a very attractive man, Miss Walsh,' the girl responded softly, sending Caryn a sidelong glance. 'You wouldn't be the first girl who set her cap at him.'

'What a disgusting expression! I'm amazed at your utter lack of manners! For your information, I did not come here for any other reason than that my doctor advised a change and a rest–' She broke off, disgusted with herself for sitting here, carrying on this wholly distasteful conversation with the girl. She rose instantly and would have gone into the house, but Harriet began speaking again, saying that it was obvious that Sharn was not troubling himself about any indisposition, as otherwise he would not be sending her back so soon.

Sending her back . . . Red-hot fury rose within Caryn at these words. Sending her back! Yes, in effect that was exactly what Sharn was doing. She recalled with clarity that first conversation she had with him. He had done most of the talking; she had almost instantly agreed with his suggestion that she go back home to England.

'I'll make arrangements for you to have an allowance each month,' he had said without at that time even having asked if she wanted an allowance. He would also give her the money for her fare back to England, he had readily promised – without at that time even having asked if she wanted to return to England. 'You'll be willing to fall in with my suggestion?' he had eventually asked, and she had hesitated no longer than a few seconds before saying yes, she would be willing to fall in with his suggestion. True, the thought of remaining among people she did not like had played its part in influencing her, but looking back now she realized that she had been given no real opportunity to think for herself and to make up her own mind. It had been made up for her, by Sharn . . .

'He thought he was doing it for the best,' she told herself a few minutes later as she stood by the small wash basin gazing into the tiny cracked mirror above it. 'I mustn't put the whole blame on him.' Nor must she go back on her word, she sternly told herself, by now having thrown off the fury aroused by that detestable girl. She had agreed to an annulment, and to accept payment for her share of the station. To draw out would be too dishonest, and apart from that she saw embarrassment for Sharn who, quite naturally, had kept secret both his marriage and the fact that the station was not solely his. There had been no necessity to disclose either circumstance, and Caryn placed no blame upon him at all.

She found herself pacing the small, airless room, her eyes downcast as she fell into deep thought. Vaguely she was aware of the threadbare rug by the bed, the spider's web by the skirting in one corner of the room.

73

The bed-cover was faded – the kind of thing one tore up for dusters, she thought, frowning suddenly and unable to think of anything else as her eyes lifted to settle upon it. This room must be the worst in the whole house . . . and she had been put into it. Fury blazed again uncontrollably, fury which she could not quench no matter how she tried. She, owner of half the vast and rich estate, to be given a room like this!

The mirror showed a face crimson with anger. Stop it! she told herself. Anger such as this was harmful to one's nerves . . .

Without hesitating another moment she went out into the corridor. The wide balustraded staircase with its exquisite carving was a long way off, at the far end of the corridor and facing a large square upper hall or landing. The stairs Caryn had been using obviously were those used by servants in the old days. She knew that the two lubras used them, their rooms being off the small corridor, as was her tiny apartment. Reaching the wide landing at the top of the main staircase, she pushed open the first door she came to – and gave a small gasp, forgetting her anger in her appreciation of the beautiful bedroom which, high-ceilinged and with two huge windows affording a view of the garden and river and the ochre-coloured hills beyond, had two doors leading off it. One, she soon discovered, was a dressing-room, the other a bathroom with a coloured suite, separate shower – and gold-plated fittings!

Standing in the doorway she drew a deep breath, then released the air slowly. Whose room was this? Walking over to the dressing-table she saw hairbrushes and a comb, a ring stand and one or two jars of some kind of face cream.

'Probably Sandra and her husband sleep here . . .'

she murmured, going over to the wardrobe and opening the door. All women's clothes. The other wardrobe contained men's clothing. 'How very nice – Fred and Sandra!'

The next room along the corridor was rather austere. Caryn knew instinctively that this was where Vic slept.

The third room she entered was Harriet's, as on the bed lay a dress which Caryn recognized, the girl having worn it at lunch-time that day. Again Caryn gasped at the beauty of her surroundings. Old mellowed furniture and a Persian carpet; thick lambswool rugs by the bed and dressing-table. This room also had its own private bathroom but no dressing-room. It looked out on to the woodlands at the side of the garden. Caryn's eyes seemed to become fixed on the exquisitely-quilted bed-cover in silver-grey satin, but she saw only the faded worn-out counterpane she had been given by Sandra.

The fourth room Caryn entered was Mary's; she saw this at a glance, recognizing the stick with which the girl sometimes walked. It was propped against the dressing-table. Caryn merely looked in and closed the door again, proceeding towards the end of this wing where the presence of two doors only denoted that these rooms were even larger than those already seen by Caryn. On opening the first door she saw that the room was not at present in use, as white dust sheets covered the bed and other furnishings. A communicating door drew her to it and a moment later she was standing just inside the room used by Sharn. It was thickly carpeted, with tapestry-lined walls and a long low window on one side and a high one on another wall. The view from the south window was on to the

75

swimming-pool and the thick belt of trees behind it; the east window looked across the wooded outer grounds of the homestead, away to the spinifex plains beyond, with the river winding through them.

She stood staring at the tester bed, imagining Sharn in it; she glanced round at the walls and the lovely Georgian furniture, at the long damask curtains. On the dressing-table were two silver-backed hairbrushes – severely plain except for the initials: S.C. Caryn had known this was Sharn's room because she had noticed him at the window one day when she had happened to glance up while strolling in the garden. Two doors led off it and she opened the one nearest to her. A bathroom, with all the essentials for a man's toilet. Turning back into the first room, she noticed two similar doors, but made no attempt to open either of them.

On leaving this part of the house she entered another wing; here was a room she guessed was used by Sharn's mother, and a further two bedrooms were unused. As in the one next to Sharn's dust covers had been thrown over the furniture.

So there was no excuse for her having been put into so shabby a bedroom, and Caryn asked herself again why Sandra should take such a dislike to her. Harriet's attitude she could now understand; the girl was so possessive both about Sharn and his home that she would have resented any woman's coming to stay. Caryn felt sure of this, especially since hearing Harriet's outspoken implication that she, Caryn, had come to Sandy Creek only because she had been attracted by Sharn. It was all so laughable, really, decided Caryn, and thought she could have enjoyed the situation could she only control her temper all the time – and of course had she been more comfortable both mentally and physically. But Laurie intruded often still, and with the intrusions a deep depression would instantly descend upon her. Then there was the matter of her bedroom. Short though her stay was to be, she would certainly have wished for a clean and comfortable place in which to sleep.

However, as there were only three or four days to go she resigned herself to the lack of comfort and of the luxury of a bathroom. At present she was having to share the bathroom used by the two lubras and the rouseabout.

At the dinner-table that evening she found herself being put at the extreme end, as far away from Sharn as possible. She hesitated, looking at Sandra.

'Why the change?' she asked. 'That's my place, next to Sharn.'

'We don't have any particular place,' came the sharp response. 'Harriet happens to have put you there this evening.'

Caryn sat down, so choked with fury that she wondered whether she wasted her time sitting at the table at all, since she felt sure she would be quite unable to eat.

However, she did manage something, but it was a miserable meal, as she was never once brought into the conversation, Vic being absent as he had accepted an invitation from one of the stockmen and his wife who were celebrating their first wedding anniversary with a party.

After dinner, when they all drifted out to the verandah to enjoy the cool night air as they drank their coffee, Fred sat next to Caryn and opened up a conversation with her.

'Harriet tells us you're leaving in a few days' time?'

'That was my intention,' she replied, astounding herself by these words which seemed to have come out unbidden.

'Was, Miss Walsh?'

'I expect I shall leave as arranged,' she said. 'The exact date of my departure depends on Sharn, and when he can spare the time to take me to the railway station at Brancorry.'

'That's where Dick picked you up?'

'Yes. I'd changed trains at Toowoomba – after flying over, of course.'

'Well, Miss Walsh, if it will help you I myself can take you to Brancorry. You see, the school's closing on Friday for three days.'

She looked at him, saw him glance in his wife's direction. Then Sandra and Harriet also exchanged glances.

So this had been planned by the three of them . . .

Caryn looked at Sharn who, totally oblivious of the tension existing so close to him, was chatting to Mary, and there was a most appealing softness about his face as he looked at his sister, and his smile was unmistakably tender. Mary had sat on one side of him at dinner, Harriet on the other, but it was to Mary that he gave most of his attention, Caryn had noticed, so it hadn't done Harriet much good taking the place which had previously been given to Caryn – from the first evening when Sharn had said,

'Come here, Caryn, and we can talk.' And Caryn had sat next to him ever since – until this evening.

Fred coughed suddenly and Caryn turned to answer him.

'It's most kind of you, Mr. Everard, but I'll wait until Sharn can take me.'

'It could be a week or more, from something he said to me this morning. There's so much work to do just now.' The man's rather characterless face was a study of feigned concern as he continued, 'I thought that you might just be wanting to go?'

'There's no hurry, Mr. Everard. I have all the time in the world.'

'You have?' He seemed at a loss and once again cast a glance at his wife. She happened to be talking to Harriet and missed the rather helpless gesture.

'Yes, Mr. Everard, I have.'

'You work, of course?'

'Not at present.'

'No? You do have a job, though?'

'Not at present,' she repeated, regarding him across the small table at which they were sitting.

He paused, and she saw him lick his lips. Glancing from him to Sharn she thought how lacking in manliness he was. There was a certain gentleness about him, though, and Caryn felt sure this would endear him to the children whom he taught.

'In the ordinary way you do some type of work?' He was now speaking for speaking's sake and she took pity on him.

'I've been helping my aunt in her shop,' she explained. 'She died recently, so I haven't a job. That's how I was able to come out here.'

'I see. But you'll have to find something when you get back, I suppose?'

'Probably,' she said and, because she had no inclination to carry the conversation further, she rose from her chair and went for a stroll in the garden, then

79

ventured beyond.

The air was dry and heady with perfume; a young sickle of a moon hung among stars that seemed larger and brighter than any Caryn had ever seen. She passed a small lake; it contained water only in the Wet, Vic had told her. At this time of the year it was merely a dry saltpan. Close beside one of its shores two bright eyes bulged from the head of a small marsupial, out hunting spiders, insects and centipedes. The tiny animal, no more than four or five inches long – excluding its tail – vanished into the protective concealment of the grass on hearing Caryn's footsteps on the path.

Caryn was strangely at peace, having determinedly thrust away the subtle suggestion of Fred's which would at any other time have proved too much for her anger. Let them plot, she thought. She would leave only when it suited Sharn's convenience to take her to Brancorry, since for one thing she did not relish camping out with anyone else from Sandy Creek – not even Vic.

The silent wilderness around her was awesome yet enticing, forbidding and yet haunting in some profound, alluring way. Turning her head, she saw the lights of the bungalows glowing in the distance, and the homestead lights that always illuminated the gardens at night. She thought of the others on the verandah, and wondered if Sharn was still giving all his attention to his sister, or whether he had turned it to Harriet who, Dick had said, cherished hopes of becoming the 'first lady' at Sandy Creek.

A sound behind her made her turn sharply, nerves tensed.

'Mary!' she exclaimed, and relaxed. 'What made you come out?'

The girl was limping, using her stick, but she was getting along very well for all that.

'I felt the need for solitude. I surmised you had gone to bed.' A small hesitation and then, 'But I'm glad you're here, Caryn.' She sounded dejected and pity welled up within Caryn.

'You're glad I'm here, and yet you came out for solitude?' She made her voice light, teasing almost.

'You're different,' Mary murmured, poking at the red earth of the bush path with her stick. Caryn glanced down, at the built-up shoe that was so cumbersome beside its fellow.

'Different, Mary?' It had never occurred to Caryn that Mary might be unhappy with her relatives, or with Harriet, who appeared to adopt a friendly attitude towards the girl. 'How do you mean?'

Mary looked at her in the dim light and Caryn frowned at her drawn expression.

'I — I like you so much . . .' Mary's voice faltered and it was clear that she regretted her words. 'Are you walking back? You don't mind walking with me — slowly, I mean?' She made a restless movement, then became still.

'Of course not,' returned Caryn swiftly. 'I shall be glad of your company.'

'You're very kind, Caryn.'

'What is it, Mary?' Persuasive tones and gentle; Mary's lip trembled and she seemed incapable of speech for a time.

'I oughtn't to talk to you, a stranger,' she began, but Caryn shook her head, stemming the rest of what Mary had been about to say.

'It does you good to talk,' she assured her. 'I found this out very recently. I talked to my doctor, because there was no one else to talk to. I felt much better afterwards.'

'I don't want you to leave!' Mary blurted out at last. 'Apart from Sharn I haven't a friend in that house!'

'Tell me about it, Mary.' The invitation came after a pause during which a surge of indecision swept over Caryn, as once again she was reminded that no one had the power to make her leave Sandy Creek. 'You can be sure I'll respect your confidence,' she went on when Mary continued to hesitate. 'Nothing you tell me will ever go any further.'

'I believe that,' returned Mary, and immediately continued, 'It's Harriet, for one thing. I'm sure Sharn's in love with her and intends to marry her. She doesn't like me and I know for sure that she'll never rest until she's got me away from Sandy Creek.'

'Your brother would never consent to your leaving. Where would you go?'

'I expect I could get a job – or Sharn might make me an allowance—' She shook her head, going on to say that she wouldn't want to be fully dependent on him. 'I do a little for my keep as things are – such as odd jobs about the house, and gardening. Sharn gives me spending money, and I don't mind taking that. But I couldn't take more – and for nothing—'

'Mary,' interrupted Caryn quietly, 'aren't you ahead of the situation? Sharn hasn't announced his engagement yet, and even if he did I'm quite sure he wouldn't marry yet awhile.' How else could she put it? Caryn would have liked to reassure Mary that the marriage could not take place for at least eighteen months. 'And as for Harriet not liking you – she seems to be very kind, from what I've seen.'

'A pose, Caryn, for my brother's benefit. Harriet

isn't like that when we're alone. She has a perfect body, Caryn, and my lameness makes her cringe. No, don't interrupt, because I'm telling the truth. She can't bear the sight of me limping about with this clumsy shoe. I'm quite convinced that once she's married she'll find a way of getting rid of me.'

Without affording Caryn an opportunity of speaking Mary went on to talk about Sandra and Fred, saying that neither of them had much time for her. It had been wonderful when she, Mary, had been the only one living at Sandy Creek with her brother. Then came her mother and there followed Sandra and Fred, then Harriet. 'It all changed when Mother came, because she took over – she's very bossy, Caryn, but not with Sharn, of course. Then when Sandra arrived it was even worse because she and Mother have always been so very close. As if these changes weren't enough Harriet had to arrive. She came as a home help, but you could see she had her eye on my brother right from the start. And she can be charming when she likes; it's no wonder he's fallen for her.'

'You're quite sure he's fallen for her?'

Mary nodded.

'Quite sure. They've gone off walking now, arm-in-arm. And whenever Sharn goes anywhere he takes her with him.'

'Does he ever go anywhere?' asked Caryn in surprise.

'To town, and sometimes to Brisbane. And she always comes when we're invited to a party or dance or film show. Everyone believes they'll get married shortly.'

'Not shortly,' Caryn was quick to assert, and the other girl looked interrogatingly at her. 'I'm sure he'll wait a while,' she added lamely, wondering how she could convince Mary that she was safe – at least for another year and a half.

Mary continued to talk, all the way back to the house. Caryn became more and more troubled, for although she was convinced Sharn would never for one moment even consider telling Mary to leave, there was no doubt in her mind that Harriet would make life so uncomfortable for her sister-in-law that she would eventually drive her away. And Caryn could not bear to think of Mary all on her own; it would be bad enough if she were perfect in body and could look forward to getting married one day, but as things were it was quite unthinkable that she should be forced to leave home – and the brother with whom she had lived since she was a mere child. Being so much older than Mary, he must seem like a father to her; most certainly he was her prop, the one person on whom she could lean.

'If only you were staying . . .' Mary seemed to utter the words entirely for her own ears, but Caryn just managed to catch them.

'You'd feel better if I were to remain at Sandy Creek?' she asked, and Mary actually stopped in her tracks.

'Oh, Caryn, if only you could! Yes, indeed, I'd feel better, for I'm sure you're my friend.'

Strange, thought Caryn, but she herself had thought the same about Mary – felt she would be the one friend she would find in this inhospitable company. There was Vic, of course, but he wasn't in the same category as the relations. He just happened to live at the house, that was all, although he had shown a marked interest in Caryn and had made life a little more bearable by

84

chatting to her and accompanying her on strolls or, as on a couple of occasions, riding with her along the bush tracks.

'I could stay a little longer,' began Caryn, when Mary broke in impulsively to say,

'You could? My brother told me just now that you were going very soon – just as soon as he can take time off to drive you to Brancorry, and that was why I felt so miserable. But— Oh, Caryn, if you really will stay for a little while longer I'll be so very grateful to you!'

Caryn looked perceptively at her, the fact clearly portrayed that Mary had been leading an unbearably lonely existence, having to be satisfied with her brother's company when it was available, which could not be often, as he had his work, and also he gave most of his leisure time to Harriet, it would seem.

'I'll stay,' she said with a sudden resolve and firmness in her voice. 'And now, Mary, are you going to cheer up?'

A brilliant smile leapt to the girl's lips and Caryn took in the change with some considerable satisfaction.

'I'm happy – very happy indeed!' she cried almost gaily, and even her step seemed to become lighter, for Caryn was sure she was not leaning quite so heavily on her stick for support.

CHAPTER FIVE

As Caryn had surmised, Sharn was not at all pleased at the idea of her remaining at Sandy Creek. He had asked her to pack and be ready for her departure on the Friday, and it was then that she informed him of her intention to stay for a while.

'But why have you changed your mind?' he demanded in a not too quiet tone. He had asked her along to his sitting-room to discuss the matter and she was standing in the centre of the room, while he was by the fireplace, dressed in tight drill trousers and a green and brown check shirt, having just a few minutes ago come in from the branding enclosure expecting lunch to be ready. But it was delayed owing to the development of a fault in the stove. 'You seemed more than eager to leave.'

'I've changed my mind, Sharn. I like it here and wish to stay and enjoy the rest and change which I originally came for.' She spoke quietly, and a trifle apologetically, not wishing to antagonize him. But he was frowning heavily and tapping the silver buckle on his belt in an angry, impatient sort of way.

'How long are you thinking of staying?' he inquired coldly at last.

'I really don't know—'

'You don't know?' he repeated, tightening his jaw. 'You must have some idea how long you'll be staying?'

She stared into the bronzed face, seeing an altogether different side to him – a harsh side, and cold.

His mouth was set, his jaw still tight. The deep brown eyes, narrowed now as they always were when he was out of doors – against the sun and wind and dust – had taken on an expression of arrogance she had never seen before.

'Does it matter very much to you how long I stay?' she hedged, hoping his answer would be such that no animosity would arise between them. But instinctively she knew she had angered him, and she suspected also that the fact of her going back on her word, after agreeing to his suggestion that she should return to her own country immediately, had bred in him an element of contempt for her. This affected her profoundly, wrenching strangely at her heart, so that she was thrown into confusion, being a little stupefied at her inability to analyse her feelings. It was impossible that this man could hurt her . . . and yet there was no denying it: she was definitely hurt by the change in him.

'It does matter, Caryn,' he told her at last, and she knew that he was making some endeavour to retain a degree of amiability. 'Your arrival was totally unexpected, and could have inconvenienced me considerably had I had visitors staying here. There really was no necessity for this visit of yours and when I suggested you return to England, accepting the allowance which I offered to make, I considered your acceptance to be very sensible. Now, however, you appear to be going back on your word, the reason for which you haven't given me?'

His tones and his manner, the way he looked at her . . . all these provoked her temper and she felt her colour rise. He seemed to have overlooked completely the fact that Sandy Creek Station was half hers. Perhaps, she thought, he had been in sole possession so long that it was difficult for him to realize the property was not his own. She said after a pause, her voice quiet but firm,

'I don't need to give you a reason, Sharn. I do have a right to be here, remember.'

Undoubtedly it was not the correct thing to say, and yet Caryn was driven by some force to put forth that gentle reminder, since she was being treated almost as an intruder. To be treated thus by the others was bad enough, but to suffer the same treatment from Sharn was something she was not prepared to do.

She heard him draw a breath through his teeth, was potently aware of the brusqueness in his voice when presently he spoke.

'Am I to take it,' he said, examining her face intently, 'that you're not now happy about the bargain we made?'

'If by that you mean do I want to establish my right here, then the answer's no. I'm quite content for you to buy me out, as we arranged, but for the present I want to say here. After all, there are still eighteen months to go before we can annul our marriage.'

He gave a slight start at her mention of eighteen months, immediately asking if this was the period for which she intended staying at Sandy Creek.

'I've already said I don't know how long I shall be staying. I did intend remaining here for that time, as I told you. Whether or not I shall decide to leave before then is a question I can't answer at present.' She was musing on the possibility that life might just become unbearable for her and that, despite her concern for Mary, she would succumb to the temptation to leave the atmosphere of disunity and return to her own country.

'It certainly isn't convenient for you to stay for eighteen months,' he told her shortly. 'I fail to see why you've suddenly changed your mind.'

'I like it here,' was all she offered by way of explanation, then added tautly, because her temper was still troublesome, and yet regretfully also, because of the rift that was fast developing between them, 'If I do decide to prolong my stay to eighteen months, then I'm afraid it will have to be convenient, Sharn. There are many rooms in this house and I would like a bedroom with a bathroom, and perhaps a sitting-room as well.'

Silence; he stared arrogantly at her and she realized that, as the Boss of Sandy Creek, he was unused to being spoken to in this fashion.

'That,' he said between his teeth, 'is quite impossible. You have your bedroom and that must suffice.'

'I see,' she returned quietly. 'It would appear that I must assert myself. I intend to have comfort during my stay here. I shall move into one of the vacant rooms.' She was very pale, and a trembling had seized her. But outwardly she retained a calm that brought an almost savage glint to his eyes. She supposed her manner appeared to be one of arrogance and defiance ... but little did he know how she really felt!

'I hope you won't assert yourself,' he snapped. 'This place is just as much mine as yours, remember!'

'It's more yours than mine – or so it would seem by the number of your people who are in residence here,' she retorted with heavy sarcasm, suddenly uncaring that the position was swiftly worsening and that they were bordering on a real quarrel. 'What I'm asking is small in comparison. Have you seen the room your sister put me in?'

'I expect she made you comfortable.'

'Do you?' She told him where she was and he gave a start, frowning as well.

'There must have been some mistake. Sandra would never put a guest in there.'

'But she did, Sharn. And I'm sharing a bathroom with the lubras and the rouseabout.'

A small silence and then, all his anger dropping from him,

'I'm sorry, Caryn. As I said, there must have been some mistake. Sandra would naturally give you a room with a bath.'

Caryn allowed this to pass. It was unimportant beside the fact that Sharn's anger had subsided. She offered him a fluttering smile, but although his face had lost its mask of harshness it did not relax to the extent of a responsive gesture, and with a sigh she turned away towards the door.

'There's nothing more we wish to discuss?' she said on reaching it and placing her hand on the ornate brass knob.

'Not at present,' came the terse reply, and Caryn left the room, tears actually springing to her eyes as she made her way to the room allotted to her by his sister. Why should she be so upset? But it was understandable, she decided after a moment's thought. Firstly, she had not by any means recovered from the upsets of the past few weeks, and secondly, it was only natural that disunity between Sharn and herself would cause her some dismay, since she had to live here along with him and his family. Perhaps she ought not to have allowed herself to be influenced by Mary who, after all, was really nothing to her.

Yet in all honesty Caryn had to admit that Mary had come into the picture late; prior to that talk they'd had Caryn had been suspended in a vacuum between her desire to get away as soon as possible, and a reluctance to leave those detestable people in possession of property that was jointly hers. Yes, there had been indecision long before the meeting with Mary out there in the bush, and Caryn half-suspected she would have remained anyway, just out of sheer obstinacy.

A small flock of emus stalked into the bushes by the roadside; two kangaroos lifted their heads to stare indifferently at the car as it went past them.

'They sleep in the daytime,' Dick explained. 'Then at sundown they move to a water-hole and after quenching their thirst they begin grazing.'

'But they graze in the daylight; I've seen them.' Caryn was sitting with Mary in the back of the car; Greg was in the front with his friend. It had been a pleasant surprise to Caryn when, the two young men having come over to Sandy Creek for a visit, Greg had suggested that the four of them go into town for the day.

'Imagine their wanting me,' Mary had said, and a quick frown had come to settle on Caryn's brow.

'And why not?' she had inquired indignantly. 'I see no reason why they shouldn't want you just as much as they want me.'

'You're so kind,' was all Mary had said, and Caryn had been set thinking of a way in which she could draw out the girl, making her aware of her attractions. In looks she was beautiful; in nature everything a man could desire. But she had convinced herself that no man would want her, and Caryn began to wonder if the idea had been instilled into her in some way by her mother or sister – or both. Certainly Sharn would never disparage her; he thought too much about her.

The car was bumping along the red earth road and on all sides stretched the plains, the everlasting plains of the Inland, the Never-Never, harsh forbidding territory, inhospitable yet challenging, a land which, with all the time of eternity to spare, seemed patiently and passively to await the extinction of man so that every trace of his presence could be erased and his temporary domain reclaimed by Nature.

In the four weeks she had been at Sandy Creek Caryn had come to love her new environment, finding a haunting solace in the isolation and absence of rush and hurry to which she had always been used. She found contentment in the vastness which itself bred peace and tranquillity. In what others had described as monotonous she perceived colour patterns that were ever new, and a delight to her vision. She likened the tiny wild flowers to jewels, the acacia-laden air to heady wine. She saw pictures in the varying shades of dawn and dusk as the sun's shifting rays lavished colour on the land – rose and coral, flaring carmine and tender cerise. She discovered a microcosm of beauty in the cloud formations at sundown, when golden edges frilled the woolpacks; she adored the jacko and his mate who never failed to appear below her window at dawn, drawing her from her bed and laughing as she rubbed the sleep from her eyes. The screeching galahs held a fascination for her, as did the exotic flowers of the garden and the supremely graceful eucalyptus trees of which in the whole country there were five hundred and thirty varieties. Caryn found their names intriguing: bloodwoods and stringybarks, peppermint and box, mahoganies and mountain ash and a host of others. Caryn had learned about them from Mary, who explained their various uses and in what parts of the continent the respective species flourished.

Mary also told her about the animals and the way the white man had practically exterminated the gentle harmless creatures because their skins were useful to him. The adorable koala had been one of the worst hit victims of man's greed, succumbing to systematic slaughter until at last he had become protected.

Every day Caryn found something new, or made her discoveries through her conversations with Mary, who became her constant companion so that the household had become divided in a way, though not in any too noticeable a manner. They all ate together, and gathered on the verandah for a sundowner.

With Sharn and Caryn a coldness had developed; she knew he tolerated her because he had no alternative, suspected he would have been delighted were she to say she had decided to leave and return to England. But the longer she remained the more she came to love the land which so many had found hostile and untameable. And she often wondered what she would feel like when the time for her departure did arrive – when she was forced to leave, owing to the annulment which must inevitably take place. There would be the subsequent selling out to Sharn . . . and her share would be gone forever. Sharn would undoubtedly welcome that day once it dawned, but Caryn was beginning to realize that she herself would be deeply regretful, for even now she was caught in the grip of dejection on merely thinking about it.

She and her three companions arrived at Warramarra in time for lunch, it being a four-hour drive from Sandy Creek. They had started out early and the sun was almost overhead by the time they reached the town.

They came upon it after travelling through mile after mile of scrub, with occasional eucalypts, dark-trunked, their silver-grey foliage gleaming in the sun. Spinifex and other wiry grass covered the red soil, its spear-shaped seed-heads rippling in the breeze.

'Here we are at last.' Dick parked the homestead car between a dusty Landrover and a utility. 'Shall we stretch our legs before getting down to food?' He glanced around accommodatingly; Greg agreed that it would be a good idea and moved towards Mary who was being handed her stick by Caryn. The couples strolled along, Caryn and Dick behind the others. There had taken place a change in Greg since her first meeting with him; he was more friendly and talkative, and she now put down his initial off-handedness to the fact that, after his long journey, he had looked forward to having his friend all to himself, when they could chat and catch up on one another's news. A woman's company had not at that time been desired. However, he had got over his initial disappointment and was obviously prepared to be friendly. This especially with Mary, whom he seemed to like in a way that could become more than mere friendship – at least, that was how Caryn saw it.

The town of Warramarra was an outpost of long unwinding streets lined with shops and bars and white houses roofed with corrugated iron. Cattlemen drove up in jeeps and utilities, tough outdoor types with eyes red-rimmed from exposure to the swirling dust sent up by numerous hooves when cattle were being mustered. The men wore their working clothes – narrow trousers and checked shirts, silver-buckled belts and spurred

94

boots. They wore coloured neckerchiefs and broad-brimmed sombreros and walked with a sort of languid swagger, making for one or other of the bars.

The atmosphere being so vastly different from anything she had ever known in England, Caryn was intrigued, as she had been on her first visit. Mary and Dick were far more casual, being used to these sights; Greg was clearly interested but impassively so, taking all in without making unnecessary comments. Watching him with Mary, Caryn was once again struck by the difference in him. He took the girl's arm when it looked as if she would tread on a large stone that was lying in the road, and when eventually they entered a café he put her in the corner by the window, ensuring that she had the most pleasant position at the table for four to which they were shown. With a little inward grimace Caryn recalled Greg's coolness with her on the journey from Brancorry to Sandy Creek. Very different was his manner with Mary, who for the first time in her life was receiving a little male attention other than that given by her brother. She was enjoying herself; this showed in her swift smiles and laughter, in the brightness of her eyes and the glow of her cheeks.

After lunch they strolled along the main street, window-gazing.

'Don't you two girls want to buy anything?' asked Dick, glancing at them in turn. 'I never met a female who didn't!'

Mary laughed.

'I'll oblige, Dick. Come on, Caryn, let's go in here and see what there is.'

Mary appeared to have plenty of money to spend and she bought herself some clothes. Caryn limited her purchases to real necessities, as Sharn had made no mention of advancing her money, and she suspected that the allowance he had offered would be forthcoming only when she agreed to leave Sandy Creek. With a tinge of bitterness she recalled the doctor assuring her she would receive a welcome from Sharn. If the man had an ounce of gratitude in him he'd go out of his way to make her comfortable, the doctor had said.

Well, it would seem that Sharn did not possess gratitude – and in fact Caryn failed to see why he should. She herself was benefiting just as much as he, so neither needed to be grateful to the other. Nevertheless, there was an unfairness about the whole business, since Sharn was benefiting now while she herself must wait another eighteen months for her share. True, Sharn was having to save hard in order to make her repayment possible, but on the other hand he was living in comfort, and so was his family.

Caryn mused for a while on the reaction to her demand for a better bedroom. She had made it in Sharn's absence and received the information that it was not necessary, as she would be leaving at the end of the week. The faces of Sandra and Harriet on hearing her state her intention of prolonging her stay! Caryn would never forget them as long as she lived. That some puzzlement had ensued was plain, but if there was to be an explanation then Caryn left it to Sharn to provide it. In any case, as far as they were concerned she was Sharn's guest, and she could stay if she wished. If Sharn had subsequently proffered any explanation she had no idea what it was, nor did she care. She was comfortably installed and although she would have liked her own sitting-room she was quite happy in the lovely bedroom she had chosen, which had its own private bathroom and a lovely view on to the front garden.

'I'd like to buy some trews.' Mary's soft voice came to her and she turned her head. 'But I always imagine I'll look dreadful in them – with my big shoe.'

'No such thing.' Caryn fingered the bright blue trews which Mary was handling. 'You attach far too much importance to it, Mary,' she ventured after a pause. 'There's no reason at all why you shouldn't wear trews.'

'You really think I'd look all right?'

Caryn's eyes glinted perceptively.

'Who told you you shouldn't wear them?' she asked almost angrily, and knew even before the girl replied that it was one of the women in her family.

'Sandra. And Harriet agreed. They said I'd emphasize my lameness.'

Caryn drew a wrathful breath and advised Mary not to take a bit of notice of what anyone else said.

'You yourself should choose what to wear. Try them on, Mary. I'm sure they'll suit you.'

Ten minutes later they emerged from the shop, both carrying parcels. Dick grimaced.

'We'd better take that lot back to the car,' he said. 'I'll wager anything you like they're all clothes!'

'We can't go about without them,' returned Caryn saucily, and actually managed to draw a laugh from Greg who, despite his more amiable approach, was rarely seen to laugh.

Later she heard him say to Mary, as they once again strolled along in front,

'What did you buy?'

'Two blouses and some other things,' she replied

casually. So she wasn't intending mentioning the trews, thought Caryn, hoping she wouldn't have a return of her inhibitions and decide not to wear them.

'I have enjoyed myself,' Caryn was saying when at last they were in the car on their way home. 'Thank you, Dick, for taking us.'

'It's been a pleasure. What say you, Greg?'

'Most enjoyable, as Caryn says. We must have another trip shortly – if it's not too tiring for you, Dick?'

'Not at all. In any case, you can drive if you wish.'

'Perhaps I will next time. I didn't suggest it this time because it isn't everyone who likes others driving their vehicles.'

'Here everyone drives them. The station utes are there for all to take advantage of, and even this car is driven by some of the men, as well as by Father and me.'

Mary talked about Greg when she and Caryn were alone later, sitting together on the window-seat in Caryn's bedroom.

'He was telling me he's been saving for five years in order to have this year off work. But he wants to do some sort of a job; he says the idle life is not for him.'

'He was very expansive,' commented Caryn, recalling his almost sulky silence in the car on that first drive.

'He chatted to me, yes.' Mary looked up in surprise. 'I don't quite know what you mean?'

'He was very quiet when we were coming from Brancorry. I gained the impression that he liked to keep his private affairs to himself. However, he's obviously not averse to confiding in you.'

Mary was smiling faintly to herself and Caryn knew

a feeling of optimism concerning the relationship developing between her and Greg. Mary was still smiling when at last she bade her friend good night.

'I'm so glad you decided to stay,' she said, turning at the door. 'Dick likes you, Caryn,' she added on a wistful note. 'I can tell by the way he looks at you.'

Frowning, Caryn stared at the closed door. It was to be hoped that Mary was wrong in her supposition. Caryn had no wish for complications to set in from *that* direction. She liked Dick well enough, but only as a friend, and should he ever come to want more than friendship she would have no alternative than to repulse him.

CHAPTER SIX

ANOTHER week passed uneventfully; everyone was busy, the women in the house and the men outside, segregating the animals into different enclosures. Calves were earmarked and branded on the thigh with the station's mark. Caryn stood one day and watched what went on. One young man, slight of build but obviously possessed of great strength, threw the calves with the utmost ease, holding them while another, older man, performed what was necessary. The calves, once thrown, lay still, fear in their eyes and the heavy way they breathed. Vaccinations against disease were carried out in addition to the marking and branding. The anxious mothers lowed plaintively and the young bullocks in another enclosure roared in sympathy.

Sharn was there, helping and leading and giving out instructions. He noticed Caryn, but his glance passed indifferently through her. His work was his life, she thought, and wondered if Harriet would eventually become resigned to this. Harriet had declared she would see that he enjoyed his money, once she and he were married. She had also said he should give more work to his employees and take time off himself for leisure. So confident the girl had been, and yet, looking at Sharn as he stood for a moment, his eyes narrowed in that characteristic way, directing operations, she could not see Harriet – or any other woman for that matter – telling him what he must do.

For a long while she watched him, unable to move even though the branding of the pretty little calves repeatedly caused her to wince inwardly. There was something about Sharn that held her almost spellbound. He was supreme in the company around him; she wondered whether it were pride that gave him such an air of superiority; she wondered also if he were aware of his inordinate attractions as a man. She compared him to Laurie, as she had compared him several times before. There really was no comparison; Laurie appeared insignificant beside this giant of the Outback, this tough and hardy pastoralist who, in eighteen months' time, would be the ruler of this vast domain, the sole owner of one of the largest cattle stations of the Inland.

He glanced in her direction again, and this time his eyes remained on her face for several seconds. She felt colour touch her cheeks, and a strange indefinable emotion was awakened – a vague elusive thread of something she had never known before. It startled her to realize that this feeling had been evoked by the steady gaze of the man who was her husband ... her husband, and yet a stranger still.

No ordinary sensation this, but an unexpected, unaccountable stimulation of a chord discovered for the very first time. She turned away at last, dazed and at the same time a trifle impatient with herself for her inability to fathom what was taking place within her. She became restless as the day wore on, and even Mary's company could not allay that restlessness.

'You're so far away, Caryn.' Mary spoke teasingly, but she was puzzled. 'Is it Dick?' she asked unexpectedly, and her companion frowned.

'Dick?' she repeated, puzzled.

Faintly the other girl blushed.

'I thought you were thinking of him,' she returned.

'You were dreamy-eyed, you see.'

Caryn looked at her.

'I'm not attracted to Dick, Mary.'

'No? He's attracted to you, though.'

'I don't know how you've reached a conclusion like that?'

'He never used to come over so often. It's a long way – more than forty miles, in fact.'

'He's not come all that often.'

'More than he used to. He's been over twice in eight days.'

'So he has,' admitted Caryn, but went on to add that on the second occasion he had come primarily to see Sharn.

'He brought a message, that's true, but his father could quite easily have sent it over the air.'

Caryn fell silent. Dick had been attentive, no doubt at all about it. On the other hand, Greg had been more than a little interested in Mary and it had occurred to Caryn that the visit could have been at his suggestion. However, she refrained from mentioning this, simply because it could inspire hopes which might not reach fulfilment.

It would be wonderful, though, if Greg did fall in love with Mary and want to marry her. Undoubtedly the two were suited, both being of a quiet disposition, and serious by nature. Marriage would solve the problem of Mary's future once and for all; there would be no more anxiety over what was likely to happen when Harriet became mistress of Sandy Creek.

The following day the two young men arrived again, and this time Sharn himself made the remark,

'There appears to be an attraction,' and he looked curiously at the girl who was his wife. 'Dick never paid such regular visits before.'

Caryn frowned and shook her head.

'He's merely being sociable.' She was in the garden, on a little seat under a tree. Dick and Greg had left a short time previously and Mary had gone indoors to change for the evening meal. But Caryn always liked to snatch a few minutes to enjoy the sundown breeze and the heady perfumes of the garden. To her surprise Sharn had come from the house to join her and he too was relaxing on the seat.

'Well, we'll just have to watch events.'

She cast him a sideways glance, noting the firm set profile. Although he had spoken casually, leaning back against the trunk of the tree and thrusting one hand into his belt in that characteristic way she had noticed so often before, she knew instinctively that he was vitally interested in her response to his words. She felt sure he was musing on the possibility of a romance between Dick and herself, and considering the consequences of such an eventuality. The marriage would have to be made public; it would provide gossip for the far-flung friends and neighbours and everyone would learn that the estate was not solely his property but that it was jointly owned by him and the wife he had never even mentioned. Suddenly it was imperative that she relieve his anxiety and she said quietly,

'I'm not attracted to Dick, and never could be.'

Slowly his head came round.

'You're sure? He's considered to be the most eligible bachelor around these parts.' Why was his voice so grim? she wondered.

She rather thought that Sharn himself would be considered the most eligible 'bachelor', but of course she refrained from contradicting him.

'Perhaps, but I'm not interested in him and I'm not likely to be – nor in any man for that matter. I've already told you that I've no intention of marrying.' She saw the shadow of a smile cross his face as she said this and she added, 'It's so strange ...' A haunting recollection of her wedding day drifted into her vision and she became silent for a space. 'I'm already married ...'

She turned away, reluctant to let him see her expression. What was this feeling – this new and unfathomable emotion which once again his presence excited?

'Yes,' he murmured, 'you're married.' He was looking at her; she felt the draw of his power and knew he was willing her to meet his gaze. Obeying the mental command, she twisted her head, aware that her eyes were shaded and that her mouth trembled slightly. Strange ... but it was not of Laurie she was thinking; it was of Sharn. So why this flood of deep dejection?

'You tend to forget it.' She found herself striving for composure. 'I suppose that's only natural.'

He nodded his head.

'That's because it's only a sham.'

'Do you forget it too?'

'Not always.' He frowned thoughtfully and a sudden silence fell between them. 'There are times,' he said at last, 'when you're forced to remember it.'

'You've ... wanted to marry?' Why was the question so difficult to voice? she wondered.

Sharn stared in front of him, hesitating over his reply.

'I'm not in any hurry,' he replied. 'I can make up my mind about marriage later.' And he added, so softly that she only just caught the words, 'When I'm free.'

Why the gap before the utterance of those last three words? It was just an afterthought, she decided, and dismissed the matter from her mind.

Sharn was speaking, saying it was time they made their way back to the homestead. Rising as he spoke, he glanced down at her with a brief smile. The sunlight slanted on his bronzed and polished face; he narrowed his dark eyes against it. There was something magnificent about him and suddenly her heart gave a bound that seemed to wrench it from its moorings. A thrill of anticipation swept through her as – with what to him must have been an entirely automatic gesture – he extended a hand to assist her to her feet.

The feel of his fingers around hers was exactly what she had anticipated – warm and strong and a tiny bit painful in a delicious kind of way. As she rose he stood still, and instead of releasing her hand he retained it for a few unnecessary seconds as he regarded her intently from his superior height.

She knew that her colour fluctuated, that her eyes were bright; she attempted unsuccessfully to control the quivering of her lips. For her it was a moment of magic, with her husband's nearness the spell in which she was caught. The sun dropping over the hills, shedding its wondrous colours over the timeless landscape, totally escaped her, for she was learning, in one stupefying flash of revelation, that she was by no means indifferent to the attractions of her husband. The word love was thrust from her conscious thought, as she would thrust away the lingering traces of a bad dream, but with insistence it returned, hammering for admittance . . . and at last it gained admittance . . .

The knowledge of her feelings for her husband was a

heavy weight on her heart, since it was quite impossible that her love would be reciprocated. This conviction was strengthened day by day as she watched him with Harriet. He took her for walks after dinner; he flew her to Alice Springs to meet some friends who were visiting the Outback town. And they went alone, even though Mary hinted that she and Caryn would like to go too.

Dick and Greg became regular visitors to Sandy Creek and the four decided to make the trip to Alice and to stay for a few days and take advantage of the numerous facilities offered for their enjoyment. Dick of course knew the town well; Mary had been only once. For Caryn and Greg it was something entirely new and despite the heaviness within her Caryn determined to get the maximum amount of pleasure from the trip, as it was most unlikely that she would ever set foot in the town again.

'I'm so glad you came – and stayed.' Mary must have said this a dozen times, thought Caryn with a swift smile as it was repeated yet once again. 'I never had such a wonderful time before. You see, no one really wanted to be bothered with me, because I hinder them—'

'Nonsense!' broke in Caryn angrily. 'You've got the wrong idea about yourself, Mary.' Faint admonishment edged her voice and Mary glanced away. Nevertheless she reiterated a previous assertion that it was Caryn who was the draw, and that Caryn need not deny it as the very fact of Dick's coming over so often proved it.

'He's only begun coming over regularly since you arrived,' she pointed out, and she turned her head away, as if she were hiding her expression, deliberately.

'However, it really doesn't matter,' she added, and Caryn had the impression that the words were difficult to voice. 'The fact that he does come is what's important, since we all go out together.'

Naturally Caryn disliked intensely the course of conversation and she changed the subject.

'Tell me about your mother, Mary. She'll be coming shortly, so Sandra was saying?'

'That's right. Aunt Dorothy and Uncle Joseph are coming with her and will be staying for a little while.'

'You get on all right with your aunt and uncle?'

'Oh, yes,' with an unusual eagerness. 'You'll like them enormously.' A small pause ensued before Mary continued, 'Mother and I are not as close as is customary between mother and daughter, but my step-father caused it all. He resented me, and I always felt he was aware of my being lame. I cried one day when Sharn was at home and he made me tell him everything. I was unhappy and this made him angry. I went to live with him then and so Mother and I seemed to drift apart.' She stopped, then went on to say apologetically, 'I expect you know all this. Sharn will have told you when you and he became friendly while he was in England?'

'I do know about your leaving your mother and making your home with Sharn,' returned Caryn guardedly.

'How remarkable it was that you and he should meet there, and discover you were related.' Again she stopped and a swift smile lit her face. '*We* are related. I can't get used to it at all. But I'm glad we are. How distant is the relationship?'

Caryn bit her lip. How difficult it was not to be

completely honest with her friend. However, it was some consolation that a deliberate lie was not necessary.

'It's very distant. We're cousins many times removed.'

'That's what Sharn gave us to understand. I don't think the others believed him,' she added with an unexpected chuckle. 'I'm sure Harriet took you for an old flame of his to whom he had impulsively extended an invitation which he never expected you to take seriously.' A rather grim expression crossed Caryn's face, but this escaped Mary, who was thoughtfully putting her next sentences together. 'Harriet was jealous of you, Caryn. Did you notice?'

Evading a direct answer, Caryn said,

'How did you get an impression like that?'

'Harriet,' replied Mary quietly, 'is jealous of any girl or woman who comes anywhere near Sharn. She'll make the most possessive wife ever – and I really don't know how she'll go on, because Australian men are traditionally dominant, and Sharn would be markedly so. He won't stand for being told what he must and must not do.'

Reflectively Caryn heard Harriet saying she would see that Sharn enjoyed his money, implying that he would have to take more time off from his work.

'Harriet isn't jealous of me now, it seems?'

'I think she's got over it,' returned Mary thoughtfully. 'Sharn's not taken the interest in you that she feared—' Clipping her words, Mary coloured. 'I'm sorry, Caryn. That wasn't at all tactful of me, was it?'

Caryn swallowed, hurt by the fact of this indifference implied by her friend, and wondering how she was effectively to suppress her own longings.

'Don't worry about it,' she said lightly, her one immediate desire being to erase the troubled expression from Mary's face. 'I never expected Sharn to take more than a superficial interest in me.'

And yet, as the days went by, Caryn found herself willing him to take more notice of her. She took great care with her appearance, wearing all her most attractive clothes. She tried often to draw him into conversation; she endeavoured to force a smile to soften the natural hardness of his features. Subtle though her behaviour was Harriet noticed it, and her animosity – which had to some degree subsided – grew in strength until she had difficulty in adopting a civil manner towards Caryn, and one day she could not resist making a scathing remark after seeing her walk up to Sharn when he was watering his horse at a bore-trough.

'Have you not yet learned that women and work don't mix with men like Sharn?' Harriet's blue eyes held an expression that was a mingling of amusement and disdain. 'He'd not be pleased at your going over to talk to him this morning. We all have more sense than to do such a thing.'

'He didn't appear to be annoyed,' returned Caryn shortly. But she was hot inside, for she had told an untruth. On impulse she had walked over to Sharn, vaguely hoping that he might take a few minutes off to ride with her – or merely to chat. She had realized her mistake even before she reached him, reading impatience in the sudden frown that leapt to his brow. And his subsequent manner had been so chilling that she had very soon found herself saying awkwardly,

'Well . . . I m-must be g-going,' and even before she herself had moved Sharn had turned from her and was riding away in a cloud of dust. Burning with humiliation and with anger against herself for her unthinking act, Caryn had walked into the bush to find complete solitude in which to lick her wound.

'You came away pretty quickly,' remarked Harriet as if fully aware of the lie that Caryn had told her. 'He couldn't have given you much encouragement to stay.'

'I saw he was busy,' murmured Caryn, wondering if the girl was in the habit of watching her movements as she had obviously done this morning.

Harriet traded her smile for a sneer.

'He gave you the brush-off. Admit it.'

Caryn's eyes opened wide. She and Harriet had exchanged words before, and the girl's supercilious and arrogant conduct had on one or two occasions brought a gasp to Caryn's lips, but never had she shown such downright bad manners as this.

'What an indelicate thing to say! Who are you to adopt this attitude with me?' It was the joint owner of Sandy Creek who was speaking, and the cold pride in Caryn's voice brought a puzzled gleam to her companion's eyes.

'Who, and what, are you?' she countered, subjecting Caryn to a piercing regard as if she would read the answer to her question in those expressive grey eyes.

'I don't think I understand?'

'Oh, yes, you do! There's something about this whole business that we can't fathom—'

'We, Miss Watson? You and who else, might I ask?'

The other girl's mouth tightened.

'Don't adopt that manner with me,' she snapped. 'You appear to forget who I am!'

110

The big grey eyes opened even wider.

'And who are you?' inquired Caryn, and added before the girl could reply, 'I believe you came originally as a home help?' If this wasn't being bitchy, thought Caryn with an inward grimace, then she did not know what was. However, she excused her conduct by remembering how very bitchy Harriet had always been with her. Up till now she, Caryn, had made some endeavour to avoid retaliation, but this time she was sorely tried. If only she could tell this arrogant creature that she was living in *her* property!

'How dare you—!' Harriet spluttered, crimson colour mounting her cheeks. 'I'm Sharn's private secretary!'

'Now, perhaps,' agreed Caryn, taking possession of a deep leather chair and leaning back luxuriously against the velvet cushions. 'You came, though, as a home help.'

For a moment fury held the girl in its grip and although her lips moved no sound issued from them. When at length she did manage to speak it was to say that at least she had come prepared to earn her keep.

'Which is more than you're doing,' she added with a contemptuous, all-embracing flick of her eyes over Caryn's slim body. 'I'm sure Sharn never intended you to stay this long – sponging on him.'

Red-hot fury surged up inside Caryn. How she refrained from exploding and blurting out the truth she would never know. She counted ten instead, and it was most fortunate that she did so, because at that particular moment Sharn entered the room, dominating it by his height and power of form and personality.

'Ah, there you are, Harriet,' he smiled. 'I've some work for you to do.' He paused, arrested by the fact of her heightened colour. His eyes straying to Caryn, he noted hers also and his gaze took on the light of perception. 'Something wrong?' he inquired. 'You two girls appear to be a trifle heated.'

'That's an understatement!' exclaimed Caryn before she had stopped to think.

'You've quarrelled?' Curiously he asked the question, his eyes never leaving his wife's face.

'Nothing of the sort,' denied Harriet with affected lightness accompanied by a smile. 'We were merely chatting.' Her eyes strayed challengingly to Caryn, who turned away.

'May I ask what about?' queried Sharn in his low Australian drawl.

Should she tell him what Harriet had said about her sponging on him? wondered Caryn, then decided not to lower her dignity by mentioning anything at all about the conversation just having taken place.

'It was nothing of importance, Sharn,' she offered at last, and he shrugged his shoulders indifferently.

'If you say so.' He turned to Harriet. 'So much paper work has piled up since the mustering began that I feel I ought to get it down. If you'll come along to my study we'll spend the afternoon on it.'

'Of course.' The smile was charming, the expression in the blue eyes designed for men alone. 'If you'll excuse me, Miss Walsh . . .?'

'Certainly, Miss Watson,' returned Caryn with acid sweetness, and once again turned away, this time from the direct, inscrutable eyes of her husband.

CHAPTER SEVEN

QUITE out of the blue came the news that Sharn was to accompany the two couples to Alice Springs. Caryn's heart seemed to turn a somersault when Mary casually imparted the information that, as Dick's aeroplane had developed a fault, he had asked Sharn if he might borrow his. But Sharn apparently preferred to pilot his own plane and rather than trust it to Dick he had offered to take the four and to remain there until they wished to return.

'Can he spare the time?' asked Caryn, puzzled.

'It certainly isn't like him to take time off just for a holiday – and especially when he's been with Aunt Jessica so recently. He was in Sydney for over three weeks.' Mary herself seemed puzzled, now she was giving the matter some thought. 'Sharn could have made us postpone the trip until Dick's plane is put right.'

Caryn nodded thoughtfully. It was certainly strange that Sharn should decide to have more time off work, especially when there was so much to do.

'Is – Harriet coming?' she asked as the thought suddenly came to her, and she found herself waiting breathlessly for Mary's reply. The girl was shaking her head and Caryn relaxed, a deep sigh of relief escaping her.

'Our aeroplane only holds four besides the pilot,' she said. And after a small pause she added, 'I wouldn't have wanted to go if Harriet had been coming with us.'

113

'Nor would I,' came Caryn's grim reply, and Mary gave her a strange glance before saying,

'It's odd that you and she don't get on. I can't think why she doesn't try to be friendly, now that she's sure you won't steal Sharn from her.'

Caryn had to smile.

'Perhaps it's I who won't be friendly,' she said.

'It never is!' protested Mary loyally. 'I'm sure you'd be sociable if she would. But she's so intolerably arrogant since Sharn began taking an interest in her. It's quite impossible to like her.'

'I agree.' Caryn hesitated momentarily. 'It's difficult to believe that she came as a home help.'

'She was rather superior, even then,' Mary said reflectively. 'I sometimes wonder if she'd come out to Australia with the definite intention of finding a husband – a rich husband,' she added with a hint of spite. 'If so, it didn't take her long to get what she came for.'

'She isn't married yet,' Caryn was swift to remind her friend.

'No, but he'll have her; I feel it in my bones.' Deep dejection fringed Mary's voice and her mouth trembled. 'You'll have gone home by then and I shall be back where I was, wondering what's going to happen to me.'

Caryn could find nothing reassuring to say, much as she wished to assuage Mary's fears. She thought of Greg and hoped his obvious interest in Mary would grow into love, in which case Mary's future would be taken care of. Mary spoke again, contemplatively. 'I can't think why he hasn't become engaged to her before now.'

This Caryn could have explained quite easily, but of

course she refrained from doing so.

'You could be taking too much for granted,' she merely remarked, her voice deceptively light, cloaking her own dejection. And then, quite suddenly and quite unbidden, an errant idea intruded, suggesting that she put up a determined fight to keep her husband. Stunned by the notion, she attempted to put a rein on its expansion, telling herself that it was impossible for her to win Sharn's love when competition in the form of the beautiful Harriet was so threateningly close. The idea grew; it had been born in the first instance by the realization that Harriet was by no means sure of Sharn, as if this were the case there would have been no cause for jealousy.

What method would a woman adopt to 'get her man'? wondered Caryn who, although colouring at her mental use of the expression, was by no means discouraged by it, since along a parallel line of thought ran that most famous of librettist's words, 'Nothing venture, nothing win'.

'What are you thinking about, Caryn?' Mary's gentle and attractively musical voice intruded and Caryn smiled as she shook her head.

'Nothing of any consequence,' she replied lightly, and changed the subject, beginning to talk about the forthcoming trip to Alice Springs.

'She was furious,' whispered Mary as the plane skimmed along the runway and started to rise. Harriet had come to the airstrip to see them off, along with Sandra and Vic, who had driven the Landrover. 'But how well she hides her feelings from Sharn! He looked a little guilty, because of that catch in her voice as she said good-bye – did you notice? How like a man not to see through her!'

Caryn nodded, glancing down. The Landrover was on its way back to the homestead.

Mary was right, the girl was furious. She had been since the moment of learning that Sharn was to accompany the four on their little jaunt.

'Surely it's going to inconvenience you?' Caryn had overheard her say to Sharn. 'There's no reason why they shouldn't put off the trip until Dick's had the repair done.'

'It could be put off,' he agreed, but immediately added, 'However, if by a little rearrangement on my part disappointment can be avoided so much the better.'

'Disappointment? Dick's been to Alice many a time; he told me himself.'

'Greg hasn't, though, and neither has Caryn. And Mary's been only once, and then it was only a quick visit as I conducted my business in a day and we flew back late at night.'

'I still can't see why you must take them . . .' Caryn heard no more, as she could scarcely remain outside the open window of her husband's study and deliberately eavesdrop.

She was still puzzled herself by Sharn's willingness to accompany them on the trip. As Harriet had said, it could quite easily have been postponed. However, she, Caryn, was perfectly happy with the arrangement and as the aeroplane soared over the tropical grassland towards the geographical centre of the continent and the oasis of Alice Springs she sat back comfortably in her seat and relaxed, her mind on Sharn and the future and the question of whether or not she could manage to bring a permanency to their marriage.

As the miles were covered the landscape changed to

a region of dry semi-desert interspersed with mallee scrub. Greg, deeply interested in the natural vegetation, was asking about the uses of the various types.

'The mallee gums are really shrub eucalyptus,' explained Dick. 'They're an ingenious example of nature's work; they arrest the drift of sand in these arid regions because their roots shoot out vertically in all directions.'

Greg was shaking his head in wonderment.

'The sand would disappear otherwise?'

'It would be blown away.' The two men continued talking and after a while Caryn and Mary indulged in quiet conversation, leaving Sharn to himself, which he seemed to prefer. He took everything in, she noticed, watching him while she carried on her conversation with his sister. Sometimes a mob of kangaroos or emus would lend movement to the raw beauty of the endless plains; at other times a lonely cattle station would appear – looking like a scatter of matchboxes among a cluster of toy trees. Sharn's interest was keenly alert the whole time and he spoke only when at last they were approaching their destination, 'The Alice', a lively, bustling and very modern town situated in the very heart of the 'red centre' and just a few miles south of Capricorn. Extending several miles to the east and west of Alice, the MacDonnell Ranges rose from the plain in an infinite variety of colourful rock formations.

Soon Sharn had safely landed and within a short time they were booking in at one of the town's modern, air-conditioned hotels.

The following day they took a trip to Ayers Rock, an inselberg rising from the worn-down plain of ancient crystalline and sedimentary rocks. The most dramatic spectacle Caryn had ever seen, the mammoth steep-sided residual changed colour with the movement of the sun, or with the presence of moisture in the air. Sharn was saying this as the five of them approached the great monolith which, without thinking, Dick suggested they climb. A short silence followed; he coloured slightly and then said,

'It would be too strenuous for us. If you want to take photographs, Greg, the best place is from over there, near those sandhills.' He pointed as he spoke, but only Greg took any notice. Both Sharn and Caryn were looking at Mary, who had turned her face away – to hide the sudden brightness in her eyes, Caryn was swift to conclude. How very unthinking of Dick! But of course he had made a quite natural suggestion really, as many people were to be seen climbing to the summit of the rock, from where there was a most dramatic view over the vast plains and the distant mountain ranges.

'There's no reason why you three shouldn't climb the rock,' said Sharn at length. 'I'll stay with Mary. There's lots for us to see.'

Mary turned, her misted eyes on Dick. He looked at her for a fleeting moment and then glanced towards the sandhills again.

'Shall we do as Sharn suggests?' Caryn endeavoured to ease the moment by using a lively yet persuasive tone. 'I'd love to see the view from the top.'

She was rewarded with an acknowledgment from Sharn – the almost imperceptible inclination of his head which indicated his thanks – and absurd as it was Caryn's day was made. She gave him a fluttering smile; his eyes met hers, fleetingly, and she saw in them a response.

'You're sure you wouldn't prefer to go too?' Mary

spoke at last, and if there was a little hurtful lump in her throat she managed very cleverly to conceal it. 'I shall be quite all right, Sharn. I'm perfectly happy just looking.'

His smile came swiftly, softening every hard line of his sun-bitten face. Caryn saw tenderness enter the dark eyes, saw him take his sister's hand in his. And she thought, 'He'll never allow anything – or anyone – to make her unhappy.'

'I'm not in the mood for climbing, dear. You and I shall take a look at the caves.'

And so it was arranged, with Dick muttering something about his being a great fool, once the three were out of earshot of Sharn and Mary.

'You couldn't help it,' began Caryn, but he interrupted her, almost roughly.

'Certainly I could help it. I've known Mary long enough to be aware of just how touchy she is about her lameness.'

'I fail to see why she should be so self-conscious over it,' said Greg with a frown. 'It seems to me that at some time or another she's had constant reminders of it.'

'I agree,' from Dick at once. 'Nevertheless, as you say, she ought not to be so vitally aware of it. The fact that she is makes everyone else uncomfortable.' He paused and Caryn knew that he was angry, both with himself and with Mary. 'I shan't enjoy the damned climb after all that fuss!'

Caryn started, bewildered by the strength of his accents and of his anger. Hitherto he seemed to have little or no interest in Mary and his strong feelings over his slip seemed totally out of place. Most certainly in Caryn's opinion they were overstressed.

He remained quiet throughout the climb and it was

Greg who chatted to Caryn. It was a relief for everyone when they were once again at the base of the rock and waiting for Sharn and Mary to join them.

'It was wonderful in the caves!' Mary appeared to have forgotten her hurt, for which Caryn was thankful. 'Tomorrow you must go, Caryn – we'll all go.' Her lovely face was animated and, glancing at Greg, Caryn saw the admiration in his eyes. 'There are drawings and paintings, left by the nomadic Aboriginals, and there's a lot more – all to do with the Dreamtime legends and initiations. They must have been a charming race of people.'

'And this was all theirs until the appearance of the white man,' commented Greg, gazing round him. 'How bewildered and sad they must have been at the great changes that took place.'

Sharn nodded, but said that the Aboriginals who remained were quite happy and content.

'They like working on the cattle and sheep stations,' he added, but Caryn immediately then asked why, if this were so, they so often went 'walkabout'.

Sharn looked at her.

'They don't often go walkabout,' he denied. 'They sometimes do so – but they return. Almost always they return.'

'The instinct to wander, passed down through the years,' mused Greg. 'What do they live on when on these walkabouts?'

'What they used to live on before we came – grubs and seeds and other foods that nature provides.'

'I think they're better off for the coming of the white man,' declared Mary, shuddering at the idea of eating grubs.

'I don't know about that,' from Greg. 'There's a

great deal to be said for the natural life, and by that I mean quite categorically the life nature meant us to live. One continually wonders if the improvement of man's brain is so much of a good thing as it's made out to be. Personally, I could live the simple life myself, and be happy doing so.' His abstracted gaze was settled on Mary's face. He seemed to be considering something of immense importance. 'I could live in the Outback,' he added and, glancing at Mary, Caryn saw the hint of a rosy blush mount her cheeks. Too early yet to make a prediction, decided Caryn with subconscious caution, but undoubtedly Greg was keenly interested in Mary. And at that moment surprising a look on Sharn's face, Caryn began to wonder if he too cherished hopes of developments in that direction.

His offer to accompany them on this trip would be explained, Caryn told herself. Having seen how things were developing between Greg and Mary, he had probably expected some results from the trip. Its postponement could have perhaps led to a complete abandonment of it, he would think, hence his reason for making sure that it did take place.

Caryn pondered on what this really meant, from Sharn's angle, and felt she had the whole picture clear when she drew the conclusion that Sharn was fully aware of Harriet's dislike of Mary and that if Mary were married and living somewhere else then the only obstacle to an eventual marriage for himself would be removed.

Her deductions naturally causing her spirits to flag, Caryn fell silent, scarcely aware that conversations went on around her. Once or twice she did not notice Sharn's glances in her direction, odd glances, as if he were puzzled by her withdrawal from the conversation.

'Is something wrong?' he inquired at last. Dinner was over and they were alone in the hotel lounge, the other three having gone for a stroll in the grounds. Caryn had had a headache and asked to be excused; she was amazed when Sharn also decided not to take the stroll. 'Apart from your headache?' he added, almost as if he doubted her word regarding that.

'No, nothing's wrong.' But her eyes were downcast and her voice tinged with dejection. The weight of unrequited love was becoming too much for her to bear; its drag convinced her that what she had felt for Laurie must merely have been infatuation, induced perhaps by her own desire to have something to offset the dull existence she endured as companion and help to her ever-complaining aunt. 'What could be wrong?'

He did not answer immediately, but looked sidelong at her, a thoughtful crease to his brow. He was dressed in a white tropical suit which gave outstanding prominence to his deep bronze colour, and flattered his lean lithe body. Caryn's eyes became lowered again; his attraction was too achingly powerful. How could she sit back and allow another woman to take her husband from her? The very idea filled her eyes and to her horror she felt a tear fall on to her cheek. Down further went her head, to be brought up almost roughly as Sharn, plainly oblivious of anyone else who might be watching, put a hand under her chin.

'Tears . . .' He seemed – quite incredulously – to be suppressing anger. 'Tears for a lost love, eh?'

'Lost l-love?' she repeated, startled into the belief that he guessed at her feelings for him, yet instantly aware that her fear was absurd.

'Laurie – was that his name?' The lazy Australian drawl was tinged with mockery, but the hint of anger came through as well. 'Time you forgot all about him. Why,' he asked as if talking to himself, 'do women throw themselves away on scoundrels?'

She swallowed saliva that caused discomfort in her mouth. Her emotions were darting about so that none could definitely be pinpointed. That she was affected by the touch of her husband's hand was one thing of which she was vitally aware; that she was being disturbed by some force that pressed her to put up some sort of a fight for what she so desperately desired ... the love of her husband, she was also vitally aware. She had tried to attract his interest, it was true, but faint-heartedly, and on his first snub, out there at the drinking-trough, she had abandoned her efforts. What kind of a woman was she to give up so easily? She was Sharn's wife and at the moment no one could take her place. Eighteen months were at her disposal ...

'I'm no longer in love with Laurie,' she told him quietly, longing to touch the hand before it was removed. He withdrew it and the frown cleared from his brow.

'You're not?' and, when she shook her head, 'Sensible girl. You were told he wasn't worth bothering about.'

'I don't believe I ever was in love with him.' She went on to explain about her life with her aunt. 'I've reached the conclusion that Laurie was merely a relief from the dull existence.' She paused and waited, but Sharn made no comment. 'Don't you think that was rather horrid of me?'

'No, of course not. You didn't know at the time that it wasn't the real thing you felt for him.'

She smiled with her eyes, wishing she knew of a few feminine tricks with which effectively to bring herself to his notice as a woman, and as his wife.

'I'm glad you don't condemn me,' she murmured. She felt awkward, and he seemed aware of this because he looked a little questioningly at her. However, all he said was,

'I'm relieved to know that you're not going about with a broken heart. I haven't experienced the malady myself, but I should imagine it could be rather shattering.'

Caryn glanced swiftly at him.

'Are you being sarcastic?' she asked. 'Or are you – er – teasing me?'

'Perhaps a bit of both,' came the unexpected reply accompanied by a slow smile. 'You're a very serious girl, Caryn,' he added.

'I didn't used to be,' she returned wistfully. 'It was the three years with my aunt.'

His eyes flickered over her face, but he made no comment on this, asking her to have a drink on seeing the waiter hovering in the background.

And for the next ten minutes or so they sat chatting, and because the interlude was so friendly and free from any trace of the constraint which had crept into their relationship, Caryn found herself becoming expansive about herself, prompted – she afterwards realized with some surprise – by her husband. She talked of her childhood and ended by an admission that she was disconcerted on hearing from Dick that so many people lived at Sandy Creek. He nodded understandingly and without thinking she said,

'When considering coming out here I visualized myself being able to have a private suite, so as not to get in your way.'

'And instead you found yourself in a tiny room without a bath. I'm sorry about that, Caryn. Sandra didn't think when she put you in there.'

He was making excuses when he knew very well there was no excuse. But Caryn put no blame on him and she smiled to reassure him.

'And you really did intend staying for a year and a half?'

She nodded, explaining that she had been off colour and in consequence had felt unable to cope with the problems of finding a flat and a job. But she broke off here and added apologetically,

'I've told you all this, haven't I, at the beginning?'

'It doesn't matter,' he said, 'carry on.'

She looked at him with a puzzled expression. Why this sudden interest? she wondered.

'I took the doctor's advice and came out to Sandy Creek.'

'I seem to remember you told me you'd confided everything in your doctor?'

Caryn nodded.

'Yes; he was the only person I could talk to at that time—' She stopped, then added, 'I had already told him about my marriage, of course. I had to, because of the change of name.

'Yes,' he murmured, thoughtfully staring into the glass of beer which had just been put in front of him. 'I expect this doctor, when he was giving you advice, told you to keep in mind that the station was just as much your property as mine?' he said at last, and she gave a small start at his perception, lowering her lashes in order to hide her embarrassment as she said yes, the doctor had in fact told her to keep this in mind.

'But it wasn't owing to a sense of possession that I came,' she said, and added the qualification, 'not altogether.'

'Not altogether?' he repeated, eyes searching and interrogating.

She went a trifle red.

'I must admit that I was conscious of the fact that I owned half of everything at Sandy Creek—'

'—and therefore you had every right to come out and take up residence in the homestead?'

She frowned slightly. Was his friendliness fading, to be replaced by pique that she was in fact joint owner of the property over which he ruled like some medieval lord?

'I had nowhere to go,' she reminded him unhappily. 'I expected to leave eventually,' she went on to assure him.

To her surprise he seemed to sense her unhappiness and his face softened miraculously.

'Drink up,' he said in a peremptory tone, 'and we'll take that stroll after all. The fresh air will most likely cure your headache.'

They walked through the grounds and out into the road. Cattlemen were coming in from the stations, and many tourists as well. Parked in front of the hotels were all kinds of vehicles – station utilities, overlanding and homestead cars, jeeps and Landrovers. Trees and shrubs grew along the main street, and cypresses towered from the gardens of the impressive-looking houses.

'It's a wonder anyone ever even conceived the idea of building a town here,' Caryn murmured, her eyes on the backcloth of mountains, dark purple in the starlight.

'Take a flat area, plus water, and there you'll inevitably get a settlement,' returned Sharn conversationally.

'It's set right in the mountains—' She broke off, shaking her head. 'It seems the most unlikely place to build a town.'

'It was very necessary to have a town in the Centre.' He went on to list all the advantages and the amenities offered. Alice was the headquarters of the flying doctor service; here was the school of the air. Alice was the centre for numerous excursions which tourists could take; it had the overland telegraph station, an open-air museum and an art gallery. It was from Alice that a network of mailman services served the cattle stations, flying from one property to another, landing on the station's private airstrip.

Caryn listened attentively, catching the very attractive tone of his low and husky voice. It was an interlude of exquisite pleasure and pain, of content and wistful yearning. She would not give up without a fight! Why should a wife efface herself and allow another woman to steal her husband?

That she was more than a little irrational over the situation Caryn was well aware, but when she agreed to an annulment she'd had no notion of ever falling in love with the stranger whom she was marrying. When he drove away on their wedding day she never even expected to set eyes on him again. But she had, and in consequence had fallen victim to his tough Australian charm. And now her life's happiness was in his hands, and she intended to strive with all her power to win his love.

Although the aim was clear the method was vague; she knew nothing of the wiles of women. But she could try to look pretty always, to arouse the first small spark of recognition, of real interest. Then surely the rest would fall naturally into place?

'You're very quiet.' Her husband's voice broke into her thoughts and she looked up at him from under her lashes and gave him a smile. What would be his reaction were she to confess what she had been musing over?

'I was thinking,' she said, and immediately went on to ask where they were going.

'We're just walking.' He smiled down at her. 'Are you tired?'

'Not a bit!' with an eagerness that could not possibly escape him. 'I could walk for miles!'

'And what about your head? Has it stopped aching?' He sounded anxious, she thought, and a great lightness invaded her heart.

'Yes; as you said, the fresh air's cured it.'

She caught his brief smile before the inherent severity returned to his mouth.

'In that case, how about a really brisk walk?'

'Lovely!' and she began to skip a little to keep up with his speed.

He said after a long, thoughtful silence,

'Tell me, Caryn, what do you think about Greg's attitude to Mary?'

The question startled her, yet she felt curiously flattered and happy that Sharn should talk in this vein to her.

'You mean – do I attach any importance to it?'

'That's exactly what I mean.'

She hesitated a moment, then decided to be quite frank, telling him of her hopes.

'I'm very sure he likes her enormously,' she added.

'You can tell by the way he looks at her sometimes.'

Sharn considered, keeping her waiting for his comment.

'I expect you've noticed how sensitive she is about her lameness?' he said at last, and Caryn nodded her head.

'She seems to think that everyone is conscious of it.'

'Everyone?' Sharn slowed down a little, turning to look at her. 'Who, for instance?'

Harriet's name naturally came to mind, owing to the fact of Mary's mentioning it. But Caryn merely said,

'Mary mentioned that her stepfather seemed to be always aware of it.'

'He was,' grimly and followed by a tightening of his mouth. 'And who else is conscious of it?'

'Who else?' she asked, playing for time.

'You said "everyone". Who else is callous enough to remind the child of her imperfection?' His voice was curt; it held anger.

'I – did say everyone,' she admitted, 'but it was merely a figure of speech.' They had left the main lights behind and were treading a wooded path into the foothills. Stopping abruptly, Sharn said, in a very soft voice,

'You're lying, Caryn. I'm not blind, and it's been plain to me for some time that Mary's not happy at Sandy Creek – not as happy as she was when she and I lived alone.' He went on to tell Caryn what she already knew – that the others of his family had not always lived with him. 'Perhaps you'll let me have the truth? It doesn't matter whom you mention; you've no need to hold back because you're afraid of saying the wrong thing.'

'It's difficult,' she began, wishing with all her heart she had stopped to think before using the word that had led to all this questioning. 'And it really isn't important. We were talking about Greg—'

'That can come later.' His tones were clipped despite the familiar drawl; they held a note of mastery that thrilled even while it disconcerted. 'I demand to know who is responsible for Mary's unhappiness?'

She moistened her lips, convinced he would force the truth from her.

'She – she didn't mention anyone else—' Caryn stopped before his intended interruption cut the words for her.

'Don't lie to me, Caryn,' he advised in soft yet sternly-edged tones. 'I want a straight answer to my question.'

With a shrug of resignation Caryn said that Mary seemed to think Harriet was always aware of her lameness. What Mary had said about her lameness making Harriet cringe was naturally left out.

'Harriet?' frowned Sharn, and Caryn saw at once that he had not received the answer he had expected. 'Harriet wouldn't hurt her feelings.'

So much for his knowledge of Harriet's character, thought Caryn. How clever a woman could be if she set about deceiving a man. And how blind a man could be! But Sharn was always so busy outside on the cattle runs that his knowledge of the women of the household was limited to what he saw at night. Caryn wondered how he would react to the information which she herself could impart, from her personal encounters with the woman. He was still frowning slightly and her lightness faded. Obviously he had no idea whatsoever that Harriet could be so hateful. And this also meant that Caryn was altogether wrong in her previous assumption that Sharn was fully aware of Harriet's dislike of his sister.

'Who else did you have in mind?' she asked, and after only the merest hesitation he mentioned his sister.

'Perhaps you consider it strange that I should suspect Sandra,' he went on, on noting Caryn's glance of surprise. 'But those two have never got on very well, not at any time. Their characters are totally different; Mary's a soft, vulnerable girl while Sandra's harder altogether. She dispenses with tact, and that's why I have felt for some time that she's been a sore trial to poor Mary who, incidentally, never complains to me about anything. She appears grateful all the time for my having her to live with me—' He frowned heavily before continuing, 'I do wish she wouldn't!' His tones echoed in the darkness, anger-edged. 'I've tried questioning her about this matter of others in the house making her unhappy, but she won't give anyone away. That's why I've asked you, Caryn, because it's imperative that I put a stop to any unkindness shown to Mary.' He paused and even in the dim starlight his profile was awesomely set and stern. 'It can't be Harriet, because she's always saying nice things about Mary, and even saying she shouldn't be so conscious of her lameness as no one else really notices it, not once they're used to it.' He shook his head. 'No, it isn't Harriet.' He looked at his wife, making no attempt to begin walking on again. 'Is it Sandra?' he demanded, and all Caryn would say was that it could be, but that she herself had not noticed any particular unkindness being shown by her to Mary.

This was true, but then Caryn had little to do with

anyone in the house except Mary, and Vic, who still accompanied her on a walk now and then. Caryn spent her time between walking the bush paths in the proximity of the homestead, reading in the garden or on the verandah, and chatting to Mary in one or other of their large, comfortable bedrooms. When Dick and Greg paid their visits another room would be used, or the garden. On no occasion had either Sandra or Harriet been sociable enough to join them.

'I believe,' stated Sharn at length, 'that you know more than you're willing to disclose.' His voice was stern but, to her surprise, resigned. 'I say this because, in view of the friendship that's grown up between you and my younger sister, it's reasonable to assume that she has talked to you about her unhappiness—' He broke off on noting his wife's swift lowering of her head, hiding her expression. 'I see that my deductions are correct,' he went on to add, staring at her bent head. 'And I know I'm also right in suspecting Sandra.'

He stopped speaking and she looked up. His expression was reminiscent of one which Caryn vividly recalled, the expression that had leapt to his face on the day of her arrival at Sandy Creek. His sister had demanded to be given an explanation after Sharn had told her to see that a room was made ready for Caryn. Sharn's eyes had smouldered and, come to think of it, they had smouldered on several occasions since, and this invariably when Sandra adopted too high-handed a manner over something. Caryn saw now why it was Sandra he had suspected of making Mary unhappy.

He reverted to the matter of Greg's interest in his sister, beginning to walk on again as he did so. 'Like you,' he added finally, 'I'm sure his interest is more than just a friendly one.'

'They're alike in so many ways,' mused Caryn. 'Both are of a quiet disposition.'

'That isn't always a pointer to a happy marriage,' returned Sharn. 'It's possible to be too much alike, in which case life can become a bore.'

She was forced to agree, but made the qualification that when two people were vastly different in outlook and interests they must eventually begin drifting away from one another.

'A wise observation,' he readily agreed. 'And that leaves us with a happy medium. The similarities and differences should balance.' He was in a thoughtful mood and Caryn wondered if he were thinking of Harriet and assessing the similarities and differences which characterized their respective personalities. As far as Caryn could see the differences far outweighed the similarities – in fact, she wondered how a man like Sharn could even consider a woman like Harriet as a wife. She supposed women saw things from an altogether different angle. Men considered other aspects— Caryn blushed in the darkness on recalling Dick's assertion that Harriet would be delightful in bed, and it was no consolation at all when in addition her memory also brought back his statement that Harriet would be a dead loss in an emergency. When a man chose his life's partner he was thinking of far more pleasant things than an emergency!

Determinedly throwing off the depressing thought of Harriet's ever becoming Sharn's wife Caryn reverted to the subject of Mary, asking Sharn if he would be pleased if Greg asked her to marry him. To her surprise he seemed unable to reply immediately, and when eventually he did speak it was to say that although he would like to see his sister married he didn't want her to make any mistakes.

'Mistakes?' echoed Caryn uncomprehendingly. 'If they're in love then how can she make a mistake?'

'We don't know if she is in love.' Sharn slowed down again and stared into his wife's face, trying to read her expression. 'We don't know if either of them is in love, for that matter.' He continued to look watchfully into Caryn's face. 'I see that you consider her fortunate to have attracted the attention of a man like Greg,' he observed when at last he seemed to have found in Caryn's expression that for which he had been seeking. 'And you'll consider her even more fortunate if he asks her to marry him.' Curt the words and fringed with bitterness. Only now did Caryn admit that she had in fact considered Mary to be fortunate in having gained the interest of Greg. Honest, she made her admission to Sharn, but went on immediately to add,

'But please don't get the wrong idea. There never was any question of my thinking that Mary should take whatever comes along – in the way of an offer of marriage – simply because, being lame, she should consider herself lucky in receiving an offer at all. To me, Mary is most attractive indeed – she's beautiful. And added to this she has a charming disposition. I feel she deserves the best.'

Stopping again, Sharn looked down at her; she saw the appreciation in his eyes, the trace of a smile on his lips. He seemed emotionally affected by what she had said and it was some moments before he managed to speak.

'Thank you, Caryn,' he said then, and an added huskiness crept into his tones. 'You're the only person – besides myself – who believes that Mary has sufficient attraction to gain the love of some really presentable man. My mother once wanted her to marry a rough, uncouth rouseabout I had on my sheep station. I would never have allowed it even had Mary agreed to the suggestion.'

'Mary would never have agreed!' flashed Caryn. 'She's far more sense than that!'

But to her surprise Sharn was shaking his head.

'Mother had pointed out the possibility of my marrying—' He broke off and a trace of humour lit his eyes. 'She had no idea I was already about to be married, nor had I,' he inserted, then went on, 'Mother went a long way to convincing Mary that, when I eventually married, there would be no place in my home for her. So you can imagine the effect on my sister, who at that time was only just seventeen. Unknown to me she had become quite desperate and for some time she managed to keep her anxieties from me. However, I found her weeping one day and forced it all from her.'

He stopped and Caryn actually found herself suppressing a shudder at the changed expression on his finely-chiselled features; it was an almost savage expression emphasized by the reflection of starlight which seemed to come from the mountainsides. 'The first thing I did was to send the rouseabout packing, for his damned impudence in daring to ask my sister to marry him—'

Again Sharn stopped, and it took little imagination on Caryn's part to picture his fury at the idea of so low a person's asking Mary to marry him. 'He never even came to me – he dared not! The next thing I did was to give Mother a piece of my mind. She never again made any attempt to force marriage on Mary. However, she had already sown the seeds of the inferiority complex which Mary now has.' He paused a moment. 'It's a wonder she hasn't told you that she's resigned to spinsterhood?'

A question. Caryn answered it, saying that his sister had in fact told her she was resigned to spinsterhood.

'But I wouldn't have it,' Caryn went on unthinkingly. 'I told her she was attaching far too much importance to her lameness—'

'You did? Caryn, I'm indeed grateful to you.'

Her whole world glowed. And as if in harmony with her lightened spirits the clouds which had been obscuring the moon drifted away behind the mountains and the whole region became showered with a silver luminescence, while the sky above was a breathtaking tapestry of celestial wonder. The Southern Cross lit the heavens and a myriad blue-white diamonds surrounded it. The Milky Way trailed its inestimable path towards infinity. A breathless hush enfolded the landscape; time seemed to have no meaning. Caryn experienced the heady sensation that no one existed in the whole wide world but her husband and herself. Surely he too must be affected by this unearthly magic? And surely she, in her new resolve to fight for what she so desperately desired, could put this moment to some profitable use. But all she could think of was the prosaic action of moving closer to him, and even this passed him by, as he was deep in thought. He began talking again, about Mary and Greg; he seemed troubled, and Caryn learned of his suspicion that Mary would never fall in love with Greg, eminently suitable though he was as a prospective husband for her.

'However, I'm a little ahead of the situation,' he added ruefully. 'We have no indication that Greg will in fact ask Mary to marry him, much as he appears to like her.' Sharn then fell silent, but after a while his low attractive drawl could be heard again and Caryn was given a hint that Mary had at one time been in love with someone else. This surprised her, as Mary had made no mention of it even in those intimate moments when she outpoured into Caryn's ready and understanding ears all that had ever happened in her life – or so it seemed, so much was disclosed. But one other thing Mary had kept to herself: the matter of the rouse-about, and her mother's persuasive tactics that might in the end have resulted in marriage – had Sharn not been on hand to prevent it.

It was on the tip of Caryn's tongue to inquire about this man whom Mary had loved, but as Sharn had proffered no outright information there was no easy opening for the questions Caryn would have liked to ask. Who was the man? And was he now married? Was he the reason for that wistful expression that at times appeared on Mary's lovely face? Caryn knew a deep compassion, sure that Mary would consider her chances quite hopeless, conscious as she always was of her lameness.

With a sudden switch of thought Caryn recalled her own conclusions as to the reason why Sharn had offered to fly them on this trip to Alice. He was expecting results from the friendship which was growing up between Mary and Greg, and he had been anxious to see it strengthened into something more, hence his reluctance to have the trip postponed. Once again she had been proved wrong, Caryn realized, and immediately went on to ask herself the real reason for Sharn's offer. It was not owing to any desire on his own part for a holiday, she was convinced of that. So why, then, should he not have let them all wait until Dick's aeroplane was put right?

It was all most baffling and she found herself actually breathing a sigh of relief when her confused searchings for a satisfactory answer were brought abruptly to an end by Sharn's saying ruefully that they weren't getting along very swiftly with their 'brisk' walk.

'Are you still fit?' he then added, 'or do you want to turn back?'

'I'm still fit,' she returned without hesitation, and an odd expression flickered over his face at her undisguised eagerness.

'Very well; here we go.' And he again walked at such a pace that she needed to trot to keep up with him. Soon, however, he slowed down. 'Sorry, Caryn; I keep forgetting your legs aren't so long as mine.'

She laughed and said she was glad they weren't.

'For then I'd be a freak,' she added, tilting her head in a gesture designed to illustrate his height. But it was at the same time a sort of coquettish act and a flattering one. Would it leave him cold? she wondered a trifle fearfully as the idea occurred to her that he might be up to any trick which she could devise – and more.

But he seemed only amused and the glance he gave her was certainly not that of a man suspecting her of flirting with him. Perhaps he considered her too sincere for such things, since she had never given him cause to doubt her sincerity.

His reaction gave her courage and once again she moved closer to him, so that now and then their hands or arms would touch occasionally as they swung them. And then another idea came to Caryn when accidentally she trod on a stone which lay among the others on the rough path they were now treading, a path which spiralled up, into the foothills of the mountains. And the next time she saw a stone in her way she deliberately trod on it so that she was thrown against him, instantly apologizing but making no attempt to regain her balance.

His hands caught her, as she knew they would; she seized the precious moment to stare up at him, her big eyes wide and appealing, filled with starlight, her soft lips quivering as if she were in slight pain.

'How silly of me,' she gasped. 'I – I don't know what I've done to my ankle.'

Sharn was gazing down into her face, as if for the moment quite unable to draw his eyes away from those lovely features. But presently he said, anxiety clearly portrayed in his voice.

'You're hurt? You've twisted your ankle?'

'It was one of those horrid stones ...' Her voice dropped almost to a whisper as she winced, leaning closer to him as she did so, and placing the palm of her hand against his chest. 'Oh, Sharn, it does hurt!'

'My dear child—' he began, when she interrupted with,

'I th-think I'll be able to w-walk when I've rested it a little while.' She had already noticed a little wooded ledge romantically placed where moonlight could slant through the trees and, as if suddenly discovering it, she pointed towards it and added, 'Over there ... if I could manage to g-get to it.' Her appealing limpid eyes were raised to his again; he swallowed hard, as if removing something in his throat and then, exceeding all her expectations, he lifted her off her feet as if she were a doll – a precious china doll – and carried her over to the ledge, setting her down gently on it and, half-kneeling, he took hold of the ankle which she herself was tenderly rubbing. His hands probed, searching for any sign of dislocation, and she made little attempts to withdraw it as he did so. Sternly he looked up.

'Keep still,' he ordered. 'I want to see if you've put the bone out of joint.'

Meekly Caryn desisted; she was feeling overwhelmingly guilty – a little bitch. This was the sort of trick which would be resorted to by a girl like Harriet, she thought, and for one disastrous second the truth leapt to her tongue, ready to be blurted out. Fortunately she bit it back, obstinately telling herself that all was fair in love and war!

But she had to say something, because the utter peace all around her seemed so filled with purity that her baseness appeared almost to defile it.

'I'm so sorry, Sharn. You were looking forward to the walk, weren't you?'

'That's not important,' he assured her gently, his fingers still probing and – all unknown to him – sending delicious tingles quivering through her whole body! 'The important thing is that you're not seriously hurt,' he added at length on a note of satisfaction as he straightened up. 'Nothing to worry about. The pain will go directly.'

'Thank you ...' Shame flooded in, dissolving the thrill she had experienced from the touch of his hands. How could she be so wantonly false? It would serve her right were he some time in discovering that she had never hurt her ankle at all.

'It's partly my fault,' Sharn was saying as he took possession of the vacant space beside her on the ledge. 'I ought not to have suggested we come this way. It would have been better had we kept to the roads.'

'Oh, no. I love wandering into quiet places.'

He shot her a strange unfathomable glance.

'You've become exceedingly fond of this part of the world, haven't you, Caryn?' His face was very close to hers; she felt his cool clean breath on her cheek.

'I adore it,' she replied huskily, deriving a little consolation from the fact that this at least was not part of the act. She spoke only the truth when she added, 'I could live here for ever. I'm going to hate it when I go back.'

'When you go back ...' He fell strangely silent after repeating her words to himself. He became preoccupied, but his eyes were all-examining as they settled on her face and he appeared to be seeing much for the very first time. He took in the charmingly-formed contours and full generous mouth, the soft grey eyes staring into his, large and widely-spaced and filled with starlight. Moonbeams flattered her hair and the long arch of her neck. A pulse in the side of his throat moved spasmodically. It was a tense moment, alive with indefinable vibrations. Caryn sat erect on the ledge, her heart beating unevenly, in sympathy with her quivering nerves and the warm swift flow of blood through her veins. What were his thoughts? Was he about to hold her in his arms? she wondered on becoming aware of his hard body against her as – by accident or design – he had come a little closer to her. He said at last, in his calm Australian voice that betrayed nothing, 'There's no need for you to worry yet about going back, not until the time comes for—' But here he broke off and his brow creased in a frown. 'Just forget about going home,' he told her firmly and, she thought, a trifle roughly. 'You can't leave Mary, you know that!'

Caryn's whole world darkened and her body sagged.

So much for the soaring hopes and the almost fierce yearning that had swept through her during these last few moments when it seemed she was about to gain some results of her scheming, the yearning for contact with his body and the strength of his arms about her, the yearning for the feel of hard demanding lips ... which would lead to the demand for more ...

He was looking at her, waiting for her reply. At last she managed huskily,

'You're quite right, Sharn, I can't leave Mary.'

CHAPTER EIGHT

THE hopelessness which swept over Caryn did not last long, much to her surprise. On waking the next morning, refreshed from a dreamless sleep, she found herself instilled by the firm resolution to continue the fight for what she wanted. Sharn was her husband; her love for him had grown so strong that she knew an almost physical ache for consummation. The idea of life without him always by her side was robbed of all meaning.

Of course, he might never be able to love her; this she was forced to admit, and should it prove to be the case then her situation was indeed hopeless. But unless she pursued the course she had set herself she would never know whether or not happiness could have been hers. Already she had made some slight progress, having gained Sharn's gratitude on account of her friendship for Mary, and he was no longer anxious for her to leave Sandy Creek. True, there was the obstacle of Harriet, looming large – Harriet who it must be admitted had a a good start on Caryn in the matter of winning Sharn's affection.

'But he's *my* husband!' whispered Caryn fiercely, and by no means for the first time, 'and I shall go to any lengths to keep it that way!'

Breakfast was served out on the terrace and as both Caryn and Sharn were up early they had it together.

'How's the ankle?' he asked, startling her, rather, since she had completely forgotten all about it.

'Oh – er – it's fine, thank you.'

'I'm glad. However, we won't put too much strain

on it today; we'll just take things easy and let the others go off on their own if they wish.' He looked at her with a smile. 'That suit you?'

She nodded happily, her cheeks glowing. It didn't seem to matter a great deal that he was being deceived. What seemed so blameworthy last night had faded almost into insignificance in the harsher light of dawn.

'Yes, that'll suit me fine.'

They were joined ten minutes later by Mary, then the other two men arrived. Sharn told them about the 'twisted' ankle and Caryn wondered how she could take so calmly and unashamedly their concerned inquiries as to how it felt this morning.

'Much better, thank you,' she murmured, noting Mary's anxious eyes fixed upon her.

'I hope it won't give you any trouble, Caryn,' she said. 'Hadn't she better see a doctor, Sharn?'

'No!' Caryn exclaimed, then blushed as all eyes were turned towards her. 'There really isn't any need for that. I've just told Sharn that it's much better this morning.'

'It isn't a sprain?' Mary still looked troubled and her brother intervened to explain that he had examined it last night and that there was nothing to worry about.

'It was just one of those uncomfortable jerks one gets,' he said, his eyes still fixed on his wife's flushed face. 'You get a nasty pain for a while, but it soon goes.'

To Caryn's relief the matter rested there, but later, when suggestions were being put forth as to how the day was to be spent, Sharn informed the others that he had advised Caryn to rest her ankle, and that he would stay behind and keep her company. Both Greg and

Dick frowned slightly, as if they hadn't wanted the party to split up. Dick said after a pause,

'Shall we all stay around for today?'

'There's no need, Dick,' Sharn told him. 'You go off and take one of the trips. After all, that was the whole idea of coming here.'

Dick's eyes were on Caryn; he seemed most reluctant to go without her.

'If she must stay behind, then perhaps I can keep her company?'

Caryn bit her lip and said there really was no need for anyone to remain behind, as she wasn't suffering the least discomfort with her ankle. But she stopped suddenly, aware of an inexplicable tension in the air. Transferring her gaze to Sharn, she noticed his set expression and the steely glint in his eye; turning then to look at Mary, Caryn could not possibly miss the quivering of her lips and the rapid blinking of her eyes, as if she were suppressing tears. Only Greg seemed detached, although he, like Caryn, was aware of the strange tension that appeared to be affecting the other three. Dick's mouth tightened and he glanced away, away from the piercing stare of Sharn.

'I think it would be a – a good idea for Dick to – to remain behind with Caryn,' murmured Mary at last, in distinctly quivering tones. 'You'd prefer that, wouldn't you, Caryn?' She managed a thin smile as she looked at her friend. Caryn suddenly recalled Mary's comments about Dick's being attracted to her. Was Mary matchmaking? wondered Caryn with a frown. But if so, why was she looking so dejected about it?

'I don't want anyone to remain behind with me. There's nothing wrong with my ankle, so I suggest we keep to the original arrangements and all go off somewhere together.' Her voice was slightly high-pitched, for she was very close to tears, tears of sheer disappointment at the realization that the day alone with her husband was not going to materialize. But she must convince Sharn that she was perfectly able to take part in whatever was to be planned. She felt so utterly miserable and guilty at having caused all this trouble, for there was obvious disunity between Sharn and Dick, be it ever so slight. Then Mary seemed to be upset, too, though for the life of her Caryn could not see why. 'Please, Sharn, let's keep to the arrangements we made.' She looked pleadingly at him, willing that stern set mouth to relax. It remained fixed, but presently he nodded, as if having considered the matter and finally decided to agree with his wife's suggestion.

They went to Standley Chasm, arriving at noon when the towering walls were flushed a brilliant red; they enjoyed a bush picnic and returned by Simpson's Gap, a place steeped in ancient Dreamtime legend. The following day they were off at seven in the morning, making a round trip of two hundred miles, visiting the lovely Palm Valley and returning through a painted landscape of brilliant red canyons and purple mountains. Yet another day was spent looking round Alice itself, when they visited the flying doctor base and the school of the air, and several other places of interest.

On the final morning Sharn and the two girls were in the lounge, waiting for the other two men to appear.

'It's been a wonderful trip, Sharn.' Caryn smiled as she went on to thank him for bringing them.

Passing this over he said, smilingly,

'I hope Alice Springs came up to your expectations?'

'It exceeded them,' she returned enthusiastically.

'I shall always remember this holiday.' She thrilled to his deepening smile, the four days in Alice having left her with growing hopes for the future, even though not by the merest hint or action had Sharn betrayed anything beyond a courtesy that came close to friendship, and stopped there.

'I must thank you, too,' said Mary, whose attention was at that moment caught by Greg. From half-way down the stairs he smiled at her; Caryn automatically glanced up at Sharn, noting his concentrated stare and the surprising frown that touched his brow. Surely he was pleased with the way things were going between his sister and Greg? They had certainly come close in friendship during these past few days. Was Sharn still doubtful about her being able to fall in love with Greg? To Caryn's mind there was much to be read into the fluttering smile she was offering to Greg at this moment. It was one of several which Caryn had noticed. She also noticed how solicitous Greg was, how eager to take her arm as they walked along – not that there was any particular need for this, as Mary could walk quite a long way before she became tired. No, it was merely attentiveness on Greg's part, and to Caryn it spoke volumes that Mary should respond in the way she did.

'So we're off.' Dick alone seemed not to have enjoyed the trip as he might. He seemed glad that the time had arrived for them to leave the town.

Thinking about this attitude of his as she sat looking down from the plane a short while later, Caryn did wonder if her own manner had anything to do with it. For Dick had shown an interest in her that was not returned. In fact, on a couple of occasions he presumed an intimacy that had never existed between them and never would exist as far as Caryn was concerned. Her handling of the situation had been subtle but firm; she had let him see that she was not interested in his flattery or his attentions.

That Sharn had noticed these advances which Dick had made was obvious because he had appeared to be annoyed that Dick should be making them. The reason for this annoyance was obscure. Caryn would have liked to think that her husband was jealous of the other man, but as this was absurd in the extreme she put it outside her mind.

Vic was at the airstrip when they arrived back at Sandy Creek. He had driven the homestead car out and after the greetings and polite inquiries regarding the holiday he helped with the luggage and, sliding into the drive seat, he was soon leaving the runway and taking the party on the last lap of their journey.

'Your mother's arrived,' he said conversationally as they drove along, 'and also your aunt and uncle.'

'They said they'd come back with her,' returned Sharn unconcernedly. 'I expect they'll be staying for a week or two.'

Caryn's heart sank at the idea of three more relatives living in the house. It had been so wonderful, having Sharn's company, these past few days, away from Sandra and Fred and, most detestable of all, Harriet. And now there would be three more. What would they be like? Caryn had already formed a not-too-flattering picture of Mrs. Gaveson, who had endeavoured to force

her daughter into so unsuitable a marriage, and whose
husband had made Mary so unhappy that she had had
to go and live with Sharn. As for the other two – Aunt
Dorothy and Uncle Joseph – they might be more acceptable, for hadn't Mary said that she, Caryn, would
like them?

And this proved to be true, much to Caryn's relief.
They portrayed a natural curiosity about Caryn, sending glances from her to Sharn and then exchanging
glances with one another, but their manner was warm
and friendly and Caryn instantly took to them –
perhaps more enthusiastically owing to the charming
way in which they treated Mary.

Mrs. Gaveson, tall and angular like her son, wore
the same formidable expression which so often masked
Sharn's undoubted traits of gentleness and compassion.
With his mother, however, there were no redeeming
hidden qualities; this was evidenced by her treatment
of her younger daughter. And even now, after the sep-
aration of several weeks, there was no affectionate
greeting taking place between the two. On the contrary, neither appeared to have the slightest interest in
one another. No wonder Mary had been so unhappy!
Well, thought Caryn grimly, she had an ally now – an
ally in addition to her brother.

Mrs. Gaveson had obviously been given certain information about the girl from England, as she waited
only until she got her alone before inquiring about the
relationship between Caryn and Sharn.

'None of us has ever heard of relatives in England,'
she went on in the hard unmusical tones which, from
the first moment of meeting her, had grated on Caryn's
sensitive ears. 'Sandra and Harriet are sure there's
some mystery?' The arrogance in the uplifted head and

the twist of the mouth were more characteristic of Harriet than of Sandra, thought Caryn, wondering how on earth she would manage to tolerate the woman as a mother-in-law – presupposing of course that she, Caryn, and Sharn ever did become husband and wife in more than name only. 'I should like to know how we come to be related?'

In spite of herself Caryn could not suppress the swift quiver that came to her lips. What satisfaction it would afford her to be able to say,

'The relationship came about owing to my marriage with your son, Mrs. Gaveson.'

Instead she said,

'I believe our second cousins several times removed married – way back, of course.'

The woman's eyes opened very wide.

'How very enlightening,' she said with smooth sarcasm. 'And how, might I ask, did you and my son discover this unique relationship?'

Colour fused Caryn's cheeks, colour denoting a rising anger.

'We were chatting,' was the crisp, non-committal reply.

'Chatting?' with slow deliberation and an interrogating stare. 'You met casually?' Caryn just gave her a rather impatient glance and the woman added, 'My son never so much as mentioned you on his return from England, so I'm sure I'm right in assuming that you made no – er – particular impact on him.' A pause and then, 'Yet he invited you over here?' Mrs. Gaveson was shaking her head in a way that served only to increase Caryn's rising anger. 'Had he invited you, Miss Walsh, he would most certainly have mentioned it to us, and also he would have made arrangements for someone to meet you on your arrival. My son is far too conscientious to leave you – or anyone else for that matter – stranded at the railway station.'

She looked at Caryn, waiting for some response, but Caryn's temper was such that she felt it more prudent to hold her tongue. For she was dangerously near to disclosing the truth, to informing this arrogant woman that she owned half of this vast estate and in consequence she had every right to be here. Also, some persistent and thoroughly mischievous and spiteful idea lurking close was that of going even further and ordering half these people from the premises. But of course Caryn pushed this idea away – after dwelling on it for a space and thinking how very enjoyable it would be to stand and watch the expressions on their faces once her information – and her order – had been given.

'My daughter Sandra and Harriet are of the opinion that no invitation was ever extended by my son to you, and that you just decided to appear, to intrude into his life ...' Subtle accents edged the final four words; Caryn was fully prepared for what was to follow. 'Perhaps you had some idea of attracting my son? Many girls have had the same idea, Miss Walsh, but he's usually known how to put them in their place. He doesn't appear to have made any attempt to have meted out the same treatment to you and we've reached the conclusion that he is allowing you to remain owing to your friendship with my younger daughter.'

Mrs. Gaveson stopped speaking at last and a silence fell between them. How difficult it was to hold back the information that could so easily throw the woman into utter confusion.

Allowing her to remain ... Caryn reached the conclusion that she was one woman in a thousand, tolerating such remarks spoken in so arrogant a manner. She said, after a thoughtful pause,

'Did Sharn ever tell you the reason for his visit to England three and a half years ago?'

Mrs. Gaveson raised her brows arrogantly.

'He did, Miss Walsh, but it has nothing at all to do with you!'

Caryn counted ten, and took a long deep breath as well. It were better to retreat, she decided, and rose from the chair on which she had been sitting. For a long moment she stared down at her mother-in-law, watching the drift of colour appear in her cheeks because of the way Caryn was looking at her, with arrogance almost equal to her own.

'Mrs. Gaveson,' she said at last in an icy, emphasized tone of voice, 'I'm leaving you because, if I stay, I shall say something I'll regret. Without cause you're adopting a most unfriendly attitude towards me, but, Mrs. Gaveson, if you knew a little more about me you would most certainly practise more caution.' She took a step towards the half-open door. 'And that goes for the rest of your family as well.' At the dignity of her voice and bearing the woman started. But her anger was evident, as also was the derision which she obviously felt as a result of what Caryn had said to her.

'You're insolent!' she flashed even as Caryn was walking across the room, putting distance between them. 'I shall tell my son that it's not convenient to have you here—' she stopped as Caryn swung round.

'Do that Mrs. Gaveson,' she recommended quietly. 'Yes, you do that.'

The words arrested whatever Mrs. Gaveson had

ready in response.

'Don't go,' she said, frowning in angry puzzlement. 'Kindly explain what you mean by that?'

A faint smile touched Caryn's lips.

'No doubt your son will give you some feasible explanation,' she replied, taking another step towards the door. For the moment such was her fury and indignation that she even forgot her own hopes and desires, missing entirely the fact that she could be seriously jeopardizing her chances of happiness with her husband. It was only later, when she was alone, that anger was overbalanced by fear of the consequences of her behaviour towards her mother-in-law. Should Sharn be faced with having to invent some feasible explanation for her presence in the home which everyone believed to be his, it would place him in a most awkward position and it was only to be supposed that he would be furious with Caryn.

And in this eventuality what possible chance had she of winning his love? With increasing dejection she owned that she would have precious little chance of regaining lost ground, and much less of attaining the goal for which she had been aiming.

CHAPTER NINE

'Sharn and Caryn looked angrily at one another across the small space separating them. With a curt demand in his voice he had a few moments previously asked her to accompany him to the sitting-room which he kept for his own private use. His eyes glinted, but so did Caryn's; his mouth was tight and so was hers. She felt that only what was in their hearts was different. In hers there was the ache of pain and despair; she was convinced that in his hardness alone existed.

'I couldn't stand any more,' she told him for the third or fourth time at least. 'I'd had enough from Sandra and Harriet – and more subtly from Fred. To take more was impossible. Why don't they like me? – that's what I want to know.'

'I admit that most of my family are difficult to get on with,' came his surprising concession. But he immediately went on to say that as she, Caryn, was fully aware of the position existing she should have admitted that it was incumbent on her to practise a little more tact.

'Tact!' she blazed. 'I've practised as much tact as I'm willing to practise! You're ignorant of what I've taken from your sister and – and *that woman*!'

His eyes opened.

'That woman?' he repeated stonily.

'Harriet!'

'You don't like her?' Sharn stood with his back to the open window, one hand resting negligently on the back of a chair. He was regarding his wife with a steely intentness, clearly interested in her reply.

'I don't really know her,' said Caryn, already regretting the outburst which had contributed to this scene of anger and antagonism that was being enacted between her and Sharn.

'A most evasive and unsatisfactory answer.' A short pause followed. 'She tells me that you went to the quite unnecessary lengths of reminding her that she came here as a home help.'

'Which was the truth.'

Sharn frowned, unable to understand her, obviously, for he appeared to be musing on her strange manner.

'I wouldn't have associated so offensive a reminder with anyone like you.' His anger, aroused by a scene he had with his mother over Caryn's behaviour towards her, and which for the first few minutes of this interview had been ruthlessly directed at his wife, had lost a little of its strength and its edge of razor-sharpness.

'I would never have said it without provocation.'

'What provocation did you have?'

'The woman's general attitude towards me.'

Her husband raised an eyebrow.

'Is that sufficient provocation for downright rudeness?'

Caryn's fist clenched, but with a supreme effort she retained her calm. Beneath it, though, fury simmered, bringing great confusion to her mind. She still desired most fervently the love of her husband, but endeavouring to eclipse that desire was the gaunt shadow of his family and try as she would Caryn was unable to disperse that shadow. It loomed like a threatening cumulus cloud, ominous portent of storm and disruption, auguring ill for the fulfilment of Caryn's hopes and desires and the success of the blissful life of which she had recently dared to dream. How could love and contentment flourish side by side with the seeds of conflict and hostility which people like Sandra and Harriet could continually sow? And even were Harriet to go – as most likely she would once Caryn was established as mistress of Sandy Creek – there was Mrs. Gaveson and, to a lesser degree, Fred. Having given much thought to the situation as it stood at present – and more especially since her mother-in-law had appeared on the scene – Caryn had, with terrible reluctance, found herself leaning towards the acceptance of defeat, which meant, of course, the abandonment of her fight.

'I asked you a question, Caryn.' Her husband's softly-spoken reminder awoke her from these unhappy reflections and she lifted her pallid face, staring mistily into his, a hard face and deeply bronzed; stern and austere and yet, somehow, faintly portraying signs of distress. Was Sharn unhappy too? But of course he must be, faced as he was with all this disunity in his household. This admittance contributed to the idea of an abandonment of her fight to win his love. It could never work out, she told herself, for Sharn's hurt would always be hers; his happiness was essential to her own, a prerequisite of her complete contentment. She sighed deeply, a long and quivering sigh which was almost a sob. If only she had never come out here! If only she had kept strictly to the terms of their agreement, what a lot of trouble she would have saved them both.

'I did have provocation, Sharn,' she persisted huskily. 'I'm not intending to repeat things Harriet said to me, but I will say this: she treated me as an outsider—'

'She had no idea who you were,' Sharn cut in swiftly and a little censoriously. 'You apparently haven't been willing to make allowances for that.'

'I never expected to be fussed over. I did expect civility on my arrival.'

'You weren't expected.' Hard the tones now, as if he were fast losing patience again.

'Perhaps that was my fault,' she was ready to concede. 'Nevertheless, I did expect a little more hospitality than I received.' She paused to glance at him. 'I always understood Australians were noted for their hospitality, especially on these cattle stations where their doors are always open to strangers travelling across the continent.' A question in her eyes brought a sudden frown to his.

'On the whole we are hospitable – anyone is welcome to a night's lodging on any of these stations. However, as I've just said, my family is not—' He broke off, a faintly pained expression crossing his handsome features. Undoubtedly this was an awkward moment for him. 'Sandra and Mother have never been any different from what they are now – it's unfortunate but true.' A twisted smile erased the tightness of his mouth, fleetingly. 'Friends and acquaintances who become an annoyance can be discarded; relatives we must endure.'

Amazed, Caryn stared. What he had said was tantamount to an admission that he would discard his relatives if he could – all except one, of course: Mary. For a brief moment Caryn gave a thought to what they must all have been like when they were at home, and she immediately concluded that, while Sandra took after her mother, both Mary and Sharn had taken after their father. Yes, he must surely have been a nice man, their father, and Caryn's brow creased in an involuntary frown as she imagined his not being any too happy in his marriage.

She said, aware that the conversation had drifted away from its original angry and unsparing condemnation on Sharn's part and seething retaliation on hers,

'You sound as if you're sorry you allowed them all to come here?'

A silence followed, lasting so long that she looked questioningly at him, unsure as to whether or not he had absorbed her words, as he was deep in thought, and frowning, and she fancied she perceived regret in his brooding and rather vacant stare.

'Mary has always been with me,' he murmured at length. 'At least, she's been with me for almost ten years. Mother came because she was ill and couldn't look after herself – but you already know this. Sandra had always lived near her and they missed one another.' He stopped and his mouth tightened. Caryn was left in no doubt at all that she was correct in her assumption that he regretted having them come to live at Sandy Creek. She supposed that as far as his mother was concerned he had been urged by a sense of duty; when Sandra and she were missing one another, and Sandra requested to come too, he would have no option than to allow it, seeing as there was ample room. And she supposed the fact that a schoolteacher was needed to replace the young lady who had left was another deciding factor in Sandra's favour, her husband being a teacher capable of taking charge of the school.

'Harriet . . .' she began, then allowed her voice to fade away to silence, aware that she had been about to voice her thoughts aloud. How was it that Harriet had come? There had been no necessity for a home help; this was proved by the fact that Harriet no longer worked in that capacity.

'Harriet?' Sharn's preoccupation vanished as if by magic at the mention of the girl's name and Caryn felt her heart sink a little. 'I can't see what it is you don't like about her?'

Caryn fell silent. How obtuse men were! But then it always took a woman to read another woman effectively. Men were influenced by the veneer, especially if it were as charming and polished as that possessed by Harriet. And men were also easy to deceive when a clever woman set out to exert her charm as Harriet had done. Watching her with Sharn, Caryn could well understand his being taken in by her, for she even changed her voice for his benefit, purring like a kitten being lovingly fondled. She used her beautiful eyes in a way that surely would hold him spellbound; she could smile like an angel. Her figure was slender yet voluptuously tempting because of the affected manner in which she would swing her hips or bend suddenly, so that her low-cut neckline revealed curves which brought hot colour surging into Caryn's cheeks. But Sharn never turned away as she did; no, he, like any other man, would always look his fill.

'I can't tell you what I don't like about her,' replied Caryn at last, aware that Sharn was moving impatiently. 'I see her from a different viewpoint from what you do.'

To her surprise he smiled at this, and she wondered if the final dregs of his anger had disappeared. However, if he had intended making some comment he changed his mind, referring to the subject that had originally brought them here, into his private room where they could talk without fear of interruption, or of anyone overhearing them.

'As I said, Mother's convinced there's a mystery, and you can't blame her, seeing that you're staying here, indefinitely, it must seem to her. I told her I'm not willing to go into any explanations, and that she must remember that this is my home, not hers.' He stopped as if expecting Caryn to remind him that it was not his home, but that it was jointly hers. She had no intention of doing so and he continued, stern-voiced but no longer possessed by the fury of a short while ago when, having been tackled by his mother about Caryn, he had been told that Caryn had been downright rude to her. 'There was no need for you to have entered into an argument in the first place. You should have used a little diplomacy—'

'I told you, I've used all the diplomacy I'm going to use,' retorted Caryn after a lift of her hand had interrupted him. 'The last thing I wish is to put you in an embarrassing position, but I'm not going to be treated as an intruder, a person who has no right to be here at all.'

'What exactly did she say to you?' he asked, regarding her intently. 'You haven't mentioned anything at all up till now.'

She looked at him with a dry expression before saying,

'You didn't give me much chance. Every time I opened my mouth to vindicate myself you stopped me by some angry interruption.'

He frowned; she wondered if his conscience smote him because his whole manner seemed to soften.

'Tell me now, then,' he urged.

But she shook her head.

'The need for it has passed.' She looked pleadingly at him. 'You're not angry any more?' Was she mistaken, or had a nerve pulsated in his throat for one brief moment?

'No,' he said, an odd inflection in his voice. 'I'm not angry any more.'

After a long pause Caryn said, her voice faltering owing to the difficulty of putting forth the suggestion,

'My presence is making things most difficult for you, Sharn, and this I don't want, believe me. Shall I go home?' Her mouth trembled and tears obscured her vision. 'If – if you decide that it will m-make for a return to – to the smooth life you knew before I came ...' Unable to continue, she swung round, intent on making a speedy exit from the room. But to her amazement she was caught, not too gently, and brought round to face her husband.

'You'd leave Mary?' he rasped, his grip on her arms ruthlessly tightening in spite of the little cry of pain she emitted as she tried to twist away. 'Well? Answer me! You'd go away and leave her, after the way she's come to rely on you for friendship and companionship?'

His vehemence deprived her of clear thinking for a space and she could only stare up at him, accepting, not without a sense of shock, that he too was in a state of disturbed emotion.

'You want me to stay?' She managed to speak at last, but the obstruction in her throat had the effect of changing her natural voice into a low and husky whisper. 'For – for your sister's sake?' If only he would deny that his reason for wanting her to stay was solely due to concern for Mary. If only he would, just by the merest hint, impart to her the knowledge that her presence at the homestead was of some importance to him too. Yet even if he should, and even if by some miracle he wanted her for his real wife, how could they be happy? She was back to the question of his family, and to the growing conviction that the time was fast approaching when she would be forced to leave Sandy Creek.

'For Mary's sake, yes.' He released her, returning to his position by the window. Behind him in a casuarina tree a pair of laughing kookaburras chattered to each other and for a while this was the only sound to fall on the heavy silence prevailing between Sharn and his wife. 'Well,' he said at last in curt incisive tones, and with what seemed almost like a threat entering his half-closed eyes, 'are you staying?'

She hesitated, vitally drawn to him even in this high-handed, arbitrary mood.

'Yes, Sharn,' she submitted presently. 'I'll stay.'

'Thank you,' he returned simply.

'Can I ask exactly what the position is now?' she said after a moment of silence. 'I mean – how much does your mother know?'

'How much?' he frowned. 'I don't know what you mean.'

'You must have told her something when she questioned you just now.'

'I told her practically nothing. As I've just said, I refused to proffer any explanations.'

'But you must have given her some sort of explanation, just to satisfy her curiosity,' persisted Caryn.

'I simply said you were a distant relative I'd chanced to meet on my visit to England, and that I'd told you to come over if ever you felt like it.' So casual; he cared not a toss that everyone was thoroughly perplexed.

'Your mother knew why you'd gone to England?' she asked, and he nodded his head.

'She knew about the inheritance, obviously.' He seemed impatient all at once and it struck Caryn that they had discussed this matter on a previous occasion. He was glancing at his wrist-watch and saying she would have to leave, as he had some work to do. 'Ask Harriet to go to my study,' he said as she reached the door. 'Tell her I'll be there in about twenty minutes; I'm just going over to the paddock to have a word with Vic.' He stopped and looked at her. 'I'm sorry if I upset you,' he said unexpectedly. 'The main reason for my anger was what you said to Mother. You told her that if she knew a little more about you she would practise more caution.'

Caryn bit her lip contritely.

'It was in retaliation for something she said to me, but I do see now that I shouldn't have said it. I expect she wanted to know what it meant?'

'Naturally.'

'What did you say?' inquired Caryn guiltily.

A small pause and then, amazing her by his outspokenness,

'I told her to mind her own business.'

There being nothing Caryn could find to say to this she opened the door, preparing to leave. But, again to her amazement, he began to speak, his words bringing her round to face him.

'I really am sorry for pitching into you like that, Caryn. Did my anger distress you?'

She met his intent and inquiring gaze and her lip quivered.

'It *hurt*, Sharn ...' This came out, slowly and yet without her being able to hold it back.

'Hurt?' he repeated strangely, his eyes taking on an odd expression as they stared into hers.

She nodded, swallowing hard. The moment was too profound for speech, even could she have found words to utter. The hush enveloping the room was deeper than the deepest silence of night. And suddenly Sharn was crossing the room; he was close – towering above her, lean and powerful and incredulously attractive. An odd little throb of joy passed through her as, seductively, she tilted her head, lips parted, eyes entreating.

For a long moment she tempted, while Sharn looked deeply into her lovely eyes, a nerve pulsating in his throat.

'Caryn,' he murmured at last. 'Caryn, I—' He broke off abruptly and stepped back, away from her. Turning her head Caryn looked into the hostile gaze of Harriet, standing there, in the open doorway. Caryn's whole body sagged as disappointment swept through her. The opportunity was lost. If only she hadn't opened that door, she thought fiercely, hating Harriet as she had never hated anyone before. Another few seconds ... Tears actually sprang to her eyes and swiftly she brushed them away. But Harriet's piercing gaze missed nothing; the lovely mouth was suddenly tight as fury raged within the girl. But she managed to retain a veneer of composure and even to pretend she hadn't noticed anything unusual, actually producing a smile as she turned to Sharn and said,

'I had a feeling there'd be some work for me to do, so I thought I'd come along and inquire. I knew you were in here—' A slight pause and then, still smiling, 'I thought you were alone, Sharn; otherwise I'd have waited.'

'That's all right, Harriet. As a matter of fact there is some work for you to do. I was going over to speak to Vic first, but—' He glanced at his watch, cool and calm and impassive. The scene of a moment ago might never have occurred, thought Caryn, her mouth trembling and her vision misted by unshed tears. '—I'll come along with you now. What I have to say to Vic can wait.' He gave Caryn a smile which meant nothing and the next moment she was stepping aside so that he could pass her, which he did, joining Harriet and walking through the hall with her towards the room he used as a study.

Caryn watched them until they disappeared from sight and then allowed the tears to fall on to her cheeks.

'If only she hadn't come,' she whispered convulsively, feeling quite convinced that such an opportunity would never come her way again. 'I'm sure she knew we were both in there, and that's the real reason for her coming. I hate her!' she cried fiercely, sheer misery engulfing her. 'I c-could have m-made him kiss me!'

But Caryn's misery was to be forgotten temporarily as she was plunged into the affairs of others. She had wandered away into the garden with the intention of going into the bush, where she could sit alone and dwell on her lost opportunity, when to her surprise Dick came up to her just as she entered a sheltered glade of she-oaks.

'Dick! Where have you come from? Is Greg with you?'

He shook his head; she noticed the grim lines of his mouth and he in turn noticed Caryn's tears.

'What's wrong?' he asked, but dumbly she shook her head.

'Nothing.'

'Do women cry for nothing?'

'Please, Dick, don't ask me any questions.' She was in a highly nervous state and, frowning, he took her arm and led her to a small hummock and gently pushed her on to it, taking a seat beside her.

'That family, I suppose?' he said, grim-faced.

'Why are you here?' she asked him, by-passing his question and hoping he would not consider he had been snubbed. 'Is something wrong?'

He nodded, and now it was his own problem that absorbed his mind.

'I'm in love with Mary,' he said, and stopped, looking into Caryn's face to note the effect of this brief item of information he had imparted. She was staring, dumbfounded, while she endeavoured to assimilate the meaning of his words.

'You?' she said unbelievingly at last, recalling how she herself had believed him to be interested in her. On the trip to Alice he was most certainly showing interest, so much so that she had told herself he was assuming an intimacy that did not exist, and in consequence she had been forced – tactfully but firmly – to let him see she was not interested in his attention or his flattery. 'What about Greg?' Why this came out she did not know, unless it was a natural follow-on after her recollections of the trip to Alice Springs. Greg and Mary had seemed to come very close in friendship and Caryn's hopes of further developments had soared by the time the trip was over.

At her mention of Greg a scowl crossed Dick's handsome face.

'He's also in love with her!'

'I thought he was.' Two men in love with Mary –

166

Mary who, so filled with a sense of her own inadequacy, had long since resigned herself to spinsterhood. 'Why have you come to me?' inquired Caryn at length, her grey eyes bewilderedly searching his.

'I really don't know.' Snatching at a nearby twig, he snapped it off. 'I don't know anything!' The twig was angrily tossed away. 'I'm almost out of my mind!' His voice seemed to break. 'I'm sure she'll have Greg – and it isn't as if she loves him. It's me she loves – but she's so stubborn—' He stopped and Caryn was sure she heard him gritting his teeth. 'If she wasn't lame I'd—' He shook his head. 'I don't suppose I would,' he growled, and lapsed into a sullen silence.

Her own problem submerged by this unexpected development, Caryn said gently,

'You're not being very explicit, Dick, but some sort of a picture has emerged. Sharn once hinted to me that Mary had been in love. I'm right in thinking you were the man concerned?' He nodded, muttering something that sounded like a question as to how Sharn had come to know about it, and Caryn said that Sharn had probably guessed. What he had not guessed, apparently, was that Dick's love was returned. 'Am I right in assuming that it was her lameness that came between you?'

'Only because *she* allowed it to! I begged her to marry me, but she said she'd be a burden to me. Well, after persevering for I don't know how long I gave up. I wasn't going down on my knees! We remained on speaking terms and that's about all. But at least I had the consolation of knowing no other man had won her affections. Then Greg came and—' He flung a hand into the air. 'He's fallen for her and she'll have him!'

Caryn was frowning uncomprehendingly.

'Why, if she wouldn't have you whom – so you say – she loves, should she have Greg, whom she doesn't love?'

Dick flushed and glanced away.

'Perhaps she won't have him. I just said that – because I'm in such an infernal temper!'

'But why? Has something happened?'

'Greg's going to ask her to marry him. So damned calmly he told me, and taking it for granted that she'll have him.'

'Does he know you're in love with her?'

'No, of course not!'

'Then you've no right to be angry with him. He doesn't know he's hurting you.'

'You're right,' he admitted, still sullen. 'But he's so cocksure of himself! I wish I'd never invited him here!'

'That's not very kind,' she admonished. 'If you've given him no indication that you yourself love Mary, then you can't blame him for concluding that he has a chance.'

He stared into space for a moment and then,

'The trouble is, I can't think clearly. I was so staggered when he said he was in love with her and it was his intention to ask her to marry him. He's taking her back to England, I suppose!'

'In my opinion you're supposing far too much. If Mary doesn't love him then you can be sure she won't have him.' But even as she spoke Caryn was recalling what Sharn had told her about the rouseabout, and Mary's desperation at the time he had asked her to marry him.

'No? That's what you think! I've known for some time that Mary's troubled about her future, should

Sharn marry Harriet. She's sure there'll no longer be a home for her at Sandy Creek— No, please don't interrupt! I know you're convinced that Sharn wouldn't allow anyone to send Mary away, but if Harriet wanted her away she'd make her life so difficult that the girl would leave of her own accord – and Sharn couldn't stop her!' he added loudly as Caryn was about to interrupt. 'You don't know just how obstinate she can be! I do, unfortunately!' Dick glowered into space. 'If Mary's becoming desperate then she could just accept Greg.'

There was no need for Mary to become desperate, thought Caryn, but of course it was impossible to convey this knowledge to Dick, or even to Mary herself. Dick was speaking again, saying that there was a small chance that Mary would refuse Greg, and it struck Caryn just how confused the young man's mind was. For one moment he was declaring that Greg would take Mary away to England, and the next moment he expressed doubts as to her accepting the offer of marriage. Dick certainly spoke the truth when he said he could not think clearly. And it was so unlike him to become heated; normally he retained a cool and collected exterior, appearing so very much the son of a wealthy grazier and, therefore, a proud member of the Outback squatocarcy.

After a little while, however, he became more himself and he and Caryn were able to discuss the matter more rationally.

'So when you were giving me all that attention,' she said during a pause, 'you were in effect trying to make Mary jealous?'

'I'm sorry, Caryn,' he murmured contritely.

'It doesn't matter.' She became thoughtful, recalling

Mary's wistful expression on those occasions when she had mentioned that Dick liked her, Caryn. How hurt Mary must have been. Caryn wished she had known then what was in her friend's heart. Mary had dearly loved Dick, and the thought of his giving his attention to another girl must have been sheer agony. And yet through it all Mary had been so sweet, her affection for Caryn remaining as strong as ever. 'I think you should have approached Sharn,' said Caryn at last. 'If he'd known that Mary's love was returned then I'm absolutely sure he'd have pressed her to marry you.'

Dick nodded thoughtfully.

'I was too damned proud at the time,' he admitted regretfully. 'When she persisted in her obstinacy – repeating that she'd be a burden to me – I became so mad that I finally left her, believing I could finish with her – write the whole episode off, as it were.' He paused and frowned and shook his head. 'How do you handle an obstinate woman, Caryn? There was I, swearing her lameness didn't matter, that it was scarcely noticeable; and there she was, insisting she'd be a hindrance to me – a lifelong hindrance, no less!' he supplemented with renewed anger. 'I'd soon come to regret the marriage; I'd become ashamed of her; I'd have to forfeit many pleasures— I could go on and on. I felt like shaking her!'

Caryn was nodding understandingly.

'The trouble is,' she said, 'so many people have contributed in one way or another to make her very conscious of her lameness and now she's got an inferiority complex.' She looked at him, waiting for some comment but he was deep in thought. 'I still don't see why you should be so concerned about her marrying Greg,' continued Caryn. 'If she does become desperate then surely it's you she'll marry – if you ask her again, that is.' To Caryn this was logic pure and simple, but Dick was already shaking his head.

'She loved me too much to marry me.' Once again Caryn thought she heard him gritting his teeth. 'If she hadn't cared so deeply she might then have considered my proposal.'

'I see—'

'You do? Clever girl – because I don't! By what obscure routes a woman reaches a decision is totally beyond my simple, masculine comprehension! For me—' He spread his hands exasperatedly. 'I loved her dearly and because I knew she returned my love I asked her to marry me, visualizing an immediate acceptance, an engagement to follow and then a wedding. All so natural and cut and dried. Was it to be smooth and uncomplicated? Not a bit of it. To my amazement the first thing she did was to burst into tears – *tears*! I ask you! She couldn't marry me, because of her imperfection. She loved me too much – and this she was to repeat over and over again during the days of my perseverence. I became heartily sick of hearing it.'

Caryn looked sympathetically at him; he was leaning forward, and he had put his head between his hands.

'If she could only be persuaded that she possesses so many lovely qualities,' mused Caryn, 'I'm sure she'd accept you.'

Dick raised his head, warming to her.

'You at least haven't hurt her. She thinks the world of you.'

'And I of her.'

'That's really the reason why I came to you, Caryn. I wondered if you could help me?'

'By talking to her, you mean?' Dick nodded his head, but Caryn was shaking hers. 'I feel Sharn should be put in the picture,' she decided presently. 'He has great influence with her and if anyone can persuade her to marry you then it's he.'

Dick hesitated, frowning.

'I hate to enlist the aid of another man.' He glanced at her. 'It's a sorry state of affairs when I can't conduct my own love affair.'

A smile touched Caryn's lips.

'It would be a sorrier state of affairs for all concerned if you allowed your pride to intervene a second time,' she said, and after the merest hesitation Dick inclined his head in a gesture of agreement.

'Poor Greg,' Caryn was saying to herself a short while later, after Dick had left her and gone over to the house with the intention of seeking Sharn out. 'I do hope it doesn't take him too long to get over it.'

CHAPTER TEN

CARYN sat with Mary on the terrace and talked about the forthcoming wedding. Casting her friend a sidelong glance, Caryn noted the glowing face, and the happy expression in Mary's eyes. This is what love does, she thought, free now to dwell on her own problem, a problem that had grown considerably with the announcing of the engagement between Mary and Dick. For it seemed to Caryn that she too must soon leave Sandy Creek.

'I still can't believe it!' Mary was exclaiming. 'It's all due to you, Caryn!'

'Nonsense! I did absolutely nothing.'

'You advised Dick to go to Sharn, and Sharn came to me and talked so sensibly and persuasively that I just couldn't any longer see the obstacles.'

'Obstacles which you yourself had created,' Caryn was swift to remind her. 'There really weren't any, Mary.'

'You're always so kind.' Mary's eyes were fixed dreamily on the distant hills, seen above the woodlands bordering the garden. In the late afternoon sun they took on a violet hue, with drifts of magenta on the highest parts. Other manifestations of approaching sundown were the slanting shadows spreading over the immense plains, plains of stippled spinifex which, seen from a great distance, took on the aspect of a raw and hostile wilderness, lonely and vast, stretching away into infinity itself. Closer too, along the winding bed of the creek, a thick belt of coolibah trees sheltered a huge flock of pink-breasted galahs but could not mask the noise they made. It drifted on the flower-scented breeze and even the jackos in the garden seemed to be listening.

How she would miss it all, thought Caryn, wondering how she had come to abandon all hope of winning her husband's love. But he had never again come near to kissing her, not as he had on that day when, just at the crucial moment, Harriet had appeared on the scene. Of course, Sharn had been extra busy these past few days, and he had had little time for anything except his work. In the evenings when they sat on the verandah others were always present. But Caryn told herself that, had Sharn desired to be alone with her, then he had only to suggest they go for a stroll into the quiet privacy of the garden.

'Just imagine Dick's using you to make me jealous.' Mary turned to her friend apologetically. 'I wanted to be cross with him about that, but he said you didn't mind?'

'That's true,' smiled Caryn, forgetting her own unhappiness as she saw again the glow in Mary's eyes. 'The method doesn't matter so long as the end was achieved.' Caryn hesitated a moment. 'Greg,' she began carefully. 'You seemed to be getting to like him?'

Mary bit her lip and glanced away.

'I feel rather guilty about that,' she confessed. 'You see, I knew he liked me and I thought that perhaps I should encourage him a little ...' She tailed off, looking decidedly ashamed.

'You seem to have worried yourself so much about Harriet, and the possibility of her marrying Sharn.'

'I couldn't help it, for I knew I couldn't stay.' Mary stopped again as her voice had begun to falter. 'That's

174

why I encouraged Greg. I – I felt that in the end I'd b-be driven to marrying him.'

'Mary dear—' Caryn turned impulsively to her. 'You've been so absurd, refusing the man you loved and thinking of marrying another simply owing to fear of the future. You know,' she added with a sudden flash of humour, 'you and Dick needed your heads banging together!'

'I know. He was proud and oh, Caryn, so very angry with me. And I was stubborn, believing he'd soon come to regret the marriage. Do you remember his suggesting we climb Ayers Rock?'

'Of course.'

'Well, that brought it home to me more strongly than ever. I could see that I'd done the right thing in refusing him.'

Caryn had to laugh.

'But you hadn't; you'd done the wrong thing.'

Mary's laughter rang out in response.

'I'm a little muddled; it's because I'm so happy!'

Another silence fell between them as each became engrossed in her own thoughts, Caryn to recall Dick's anger on the occasion just mentioned by Mary, anger both at his own slip and at Mary's reaction. Yes, so much was explained now that Caryn had learned of his love for Mary. Dick must have suffered just as much as Mary had done, hurting her as he had – although quite unintentionally.

Mary was talking again, saying she would miss Caryn but immediately promising to come over often.

'Dick says I must learn to drive the car,' she went on, excitement creeping into her voice. 'Sharn suggested it several times, but I wouldn't listen.' She stared dreamily in front of her. 'Isn't it strange, but you'll do as your husband tells you but not as anyone else—' Mary broke off, flushing swiftly. 'He's not my husband yet,' she supplemented unnecessarily, and Caryn had to laugh again. 'As I was saying,' continued Mary rather hurriedly, 'I'll come over often. And you must come to us. Sharn will bring you every time he comes to visit us.'

Caryn swallowed.

'I shan't be here much longer,' she reminded her, and Mary's face clouded.

'I can't imagine not having you for my friend.' She shook her head. 'It'll be Harriet who'll be coming, and I shall have to be civil to her, I suppose. But I shan't be sisterly – not even to please my brother. Did you see her face when Sharn announced our engagement?'

'I certainly did.' Caryn's voice was edged with real fury and her grey eyes flashed. 'I should think everyone present noticed.' Except Sharn, she thought dejectedly. He never saw anything unpleasant where Harriet was concerned.

'She never made any effort to hide her astonishment that a man like Dick should want to marry me. And her congratulations were so cold and meaningless. She sneered, too, and gave me that awful look – flickering her eyes down to my foot.'

'Well, it didn't worry you, I hope?'

'I was too happy. Oh, Caryn, isn't Dick wonderful?'

'He's a very lucky man, I know that!' It was Dick himself speaking and both girls turned swiftly. Having come up noiselessly behind them, he had stood for a few seconds – just long enough to hear his fiancée's enthusiastic question, which was in effect a statement. 'Can a mere male intrude – or shall I go and find my own kind?'

'No, you must stay.' Caryn got up at once. 'I was just going—'

'No, you weren't,' interrupted Mary. 'There isn't any need for you to go just because Dick's come.'

'Sit down, Caryn,' urged Dick, taking a seat beside Mary. 'I'm not staying more than ten minutes or so. I came over to bring a couple of films I'd promised your aunt and uncle,' he told Mary. 'They've been taking that many snapshots that they've used up all the films they brought. I promised them a couple so I thought I'd come over with them, as I had an hour or two to spare.'

'All this way just to bring a couple of films?' Caryn looked teasingly at him. 'You could have given them the films on Friday, when we all came over to your place for the barbecue.'

'So I could.' He grinned sheepishly and allowed his eyes to settle on his fiancée's happy face. 'I quite forgot I was seeing them on Friday.'

'Fibber,' accused Mary. 'You just made the films an excuse – so you could see me!'

'I don't deny it, my love – although I don't really need an excuse. Had there been no films to deliver I'd have come just the same.'

Mary blushed and murmured something inaudible; Caryn felt out of it and stirred uneasily. With swift perception Dick noticed and brought her into the conversation, asking what they were talking about when he had interrupted them.

'That horrid Harriet,' submitted Mary before Caryn could speak. 'I was saying to Caryn that I'd extend civility, and nothing more – when Sharn brings her to visit us, that is. I'm never, *never* going to regard her as a sister!'

'Nor I,' grimly from Dick, who was shaking his head. 'You seem very sure he'll marry her.'

'I wish I could think he wouldn't. My brother deserves someone much better than her.' A small silence and then, 'It's her beauty that attracts him – and of course, her scheming. She flirts with him just whenever the opportunity arises.'

'I don't think her flirting greatly affects your brother. No, if he does marry her it'll be more with the thought of an heir in mind than anything else.'

'How very indelicate!' protested Mary, but Dick only laughed. He was looking at Caryn and both he and she were recalling the remark he had made about Harriet's being 'delightful in bed'.

Was that all Sharn thought about? Caryn wondered. She could not bring herself to accept this, and yet what else could he see in the girl?

'I keep forgetting,' whispered Caryn to herself, 'that he sees only her best side, the charming cover she dons for him alone.'

Dick and Mary were talking to each other again; Caryn rose, and this time she did insist on leaving them alone.

All the far-flung friends and neighbours flocked to Sandy Creek for the wedding, which took place only a fortnight after the engagement was announced. He had waited long enough, Dick said, and although this meant a great deal of hurried preparations everything was ready in the end and the wedding went off without a hitch. In the early evening the newly-married couple flew to Proserpine, from where they were boarding a luxury launch which would take them to one of the lovely Barrier Reef islands.

'You'll still be here when we get back? You promised.' Mary was just a little tearful as she snatched a moment with Caryn before she left. Dressed in a perfectly-cut suit of sapphire linen, with white shoes and bag and gloves, Mary looked adorable, and no one seemed to take a scrap of notice of the one shoe, heavily built up. Most certainly her bridegroom didn't notice. He had eyes only for her lovely face, aglow with the kind of happiness that love alone can bring.

'Yes, I shall still be here.' Caryn would have liked to leave as soon as possible after the wedding, but for the sake of her new sister-in-law's happiness she had readily made the promise asked for.

'Good-bye.'

'Good-bye, Mary; have a wonderful time.'

Everyone went to the airstrip to see them off. On the way back Harriet got into the seat beside Sharn, who was driving the homestead car. The rest of his family piled in, filling the car. Caryn felt lost, shut out. Turning from the half-sneering face of Harriet she glanced up at the aeroplane, disappearing rapidly in the pearl-grey light of approaching dusk. Mary had been her one real friend in all this inhospitable place. Caryn watched the plane growing smaller, and she felt a terrible lump rise in her throat.

'Can I give you a lift?' She twisted round to see Greg, who was sitting at the wheel of a utility, his head half out of the side window.

'Thank you.' She got in and the vehicle moved forward.

'Happy couple.' Abrupt words, and on turning her head Caryn noted his tight lips, and the swallowing movement in his throat.

'They've been in love for a long time,' she said.

'I didn't know that – not until I'd fallen for her.' He flicked Caryn a swift sideways glance. 'You knew – so I'm not trying to deny it or to cover up.'

She felt sorry for him and yet she knew instinctively that there was an element of pity in what he felt for Mary.

'It'll fade – the hurt, I mean,' she told him, and he gave her another glance.

'Been in love yourself, have you?'

'Yes,' she returned frankly, 'I have.'

They reached the homestead and joined the others who had arrived before them. Sharn was pouring drinks. He looked at his wife across the room and smiled.

'What are you having, Caryn?' he asked, and something in his manner seemed to be inviting and she was impelled to cross the room to him. He gave her the drink and their hands touched.

'Thank you, Sharn.' She was conscious of hostile eyes on her and she turned. Harriet, Sandra and Mrs. Gaveson were watching her and Sharn. 'I'll – I'll sit over here.' It was an invitation and he accepted it, taking a seat beside her.

'It was a lovely wedding,' she said awkwardly, and he nodded. Was he, like her, seeing another wedding – in a musty office in the High Street of a busy market town?

'Do you want to dance?' Sharn asked a little later, after they had spent a few moments in casual conversation, discussing the wedding and the events leading up to it. 'Or would you prefer some fresh air?'

'Fresh air?' Her heart seemed to leap right into her throat. 'Outside?'

He smiled at her in some amusement.

'The fresh air I'm talking about does happen to be outside,' he said, and Caryn's heart gave another leap.

'You mean,' she faltered, 'that you w-want to take a walk?'

'That's the idea.'

'All right.'

His amused smile deepened at her awkwardness.

'Get a wrap,' he said, and she went off, up to her room. Vaguely she noticed a suitcase on a chair, a suitcase that wasn't hers. But she had no time for investigations and, grabbing a white woollen cape, she ran downstairs again. Having left the large hall where the musicians were now playing for the guests who wished to dance, Sharn was waiting at the bottom of the wide staircase. Within minutes they were moving away from the homestead, and the music began to fade with the distance they covered.

'Sharn,' breathed Caryn, unable to trot along beside him and say nothing. 'Sharn . . .'

'Yes?' Glancing down, he took in her heightened colour, the tremulous movement of her mouth. 'Yes, Caryn?'

'I don't understand.' She looked pleadingly at him. 'You – you seem – seem different . . .'

'I am different.' The non-committal reply was all he offered for the moment and once again they walked along in silence. Only when they were well away from the homestead with its lights and music and gay gathering did he stop, on the edge of a wooden enclosure. 'One thing—' His voice seemed abrupt, demanding. 'am I right in assuming that you care for me?'

'Care?' she repeated, almost unable to speak at all

because of the staggering idea that had flashed across her mind.

'Do you love me, Caryn?' he asked gently, and even before she answered his firm muscular hands had taken possession of hers. 'Tell me – say it.'

'I – I–' She broke off, too full to speak. 'I don't know how it's come about,' she said, almost tearfully. This was too much; she was too achingly, yearningly affected and the relief of tears would have been welcome.

'Nor I,' he owned, 'but it has. Surely you knew, that day in my study? That was when it came to us – remember?'

'To us . . .' Automatically she shook her head, scarcely aware of what she said as she continued, 'To you, perhaps–' and then she stopped and looked up at him. 'Yes, I remember,' she answered, and brushed a hand across her eyes, removing the moisture so that she could see him more clearly.

'Darling . . . did it happen before that?'

She nodded.

'I tried to flirt with you in Alice,' she informed him absurdly. 'I wanted you to notice me. I didn't hurt my ankle at all–' Again she stopped. 'I'm very sorry,' she ended, and all she heard for a moment was his soft, amused laughter falling on the still scented air of the garden.

'Dearest, it doesn't matter when it happened, or whether you tried to flirt with me–' He drew her close, his hands moving to her slender waist. 'It's happened, and that is the only important thing. I adore you, Caryn . . . my dear wife . . .' His words died as his lips found hers; several silent moments elapsed before he spoke again. 'Do you remember once asking me if I'd

ever wanted to marry – marry someone else, of course?'
Caryn nodded and he went on, 'I said I wasn't in any
hurry, if you remember? I said I could make up my
mind later.'

'Yes, I do remember. I was puzzled because you
hesitated before saying, "when I'm free".'

He nodded reflectively.

'It was at that moment that I begun to notice you, I
think. I suddenly had the first faint doubt about de-
siring my freedom.'

'Oh . . . I wish I'd known!'

He frowned.

'You didn't love me then – you couldn't have.'

'No, but like you, I was – was – how can I explain? I
was *feeling* something,' she ended, and Sharn gave a
laugh.

'Well, although it's not a very romantic way of putting it at least it's not ambiguous.'

'It was only a short time later that I did realize I was
beginning to fall in love. It was when you held my
hand to help me up—' She stopped at his puzzled expression. 'It doesn't matter,' she added hastily, real-
izing that her explanation was far from necessary
anyway. As Sharn had just said, it didn't matter when
it happened. The only important thing was that it *had*
happened.

But to Caryn it was still a miracle, and she began to
tell him of her unhappiness when it seemed that she
must decide to leave Sandy Creek.

'I couldn't have endured seeing you with Harriet
much longer. Everyone thought you'd marry her.' Including the girl herself, Caryn could have added, but
naturally she refrained. She didn't want to talk about
Harriet anyway.

183

'I might have married her, eventually, had you not turned up.' He stopped and a heavy frown creased his brow. 'A man thinks of marriage eventually; he feels he must do something about getting himself a son.'

Just what Dick had said, reflected Caryn.

'You never felt anything for her?' Caryn hadn't meant to ask that, but the question just came out unbidden.

'Nothing important.' The casual tone was all Caryn needed to set her mind entirely at rest even had he not gone on to say, 'Nothing like this wonderful thing that's happened to me—' He swept her into the whirlpool of his ardour and she could only cling breathlessly, surrendering her eager lips to his hard demanding mouth, and gasping for air as soon as soon as she was released. 'Dearest,' he whispered close to her ear, 'I love you to distraction!'

'I love you,' she responded simply, and was once more drawn into the vortex of his passion.

'To think, I've had my wife close, my dear sweet wife – and did not discover sooner just how much I wanted her.'

She blushed rosily in the shadows, and nestled comfortably against him, her heart beating rapidly and joyously in intimate nearness to his.

'Tell me,' he said after a long while, 'what made you decide to stay – after having agreed to leave?'

She began to tell him that it was entirely because of Mary, then in all honesty confessed that the idea of leaving his family in possession had also proved a strong deciding factor.

'But I'll get used to them, I promise,' she went on to add swiftly. 'I'll try very hard—'

'My child, you'll do no such thing. They're going –

all of them, including Harriet!' His voice was hard suddenly. 'I'd been coming to the end of my patience for some time, and they'd have been told to go before very long. But now their departure's been brought forward. Why do you think I held back from telling you I loved you?'

'Held back?'

'I knew how I felt that day in my study. If Harriet hadn't come along—' He stopped and looked deeply into her eyes. 'You know what would have happened, don't you?'

'You'd have – have kissed me,' she answered shyly, and her husband gave a low laugh and caught her to him, tenderly.

'And told you just how much I loved you, my darling.' For a long moment there was silence between them, while he caressed her cheeks with his lips, and her mouth and her throat. 'Yes, I would have told you how much I loved you,' he repeated at last. 'This would naturally have led to the disclosure of our marriage, and to the fact that you were joint owner of this property. I should have informed them all that, as you were now taking your place as mistress of Sandy Creek, they must leave. Mother still has her house and Fred has his too. They're both let to tenants who, I suppose, will have to get out. I'm not interested. However,' Sharn went on after a short pause, 'I was in fact to be grateful for that interruption of Harriet's, as had I revealed all about you and me at that time there would have undoubtedly been some disunity in the house—' He broke off on noting his wife's changing expression. 'I know you've not had a very happy time, dearest,' he continued presently. 'But we'll soon have the house to ourselves. As I was saying, there would have been disunity — and no small amount of hostility towards you. Everything and everyone would have been upset. Well, when Dick came along with his news, and after I'd persuaded Mary to marry him, I was glad that my disclosure had never been made.' He paused and Caryn put in,

'You didn't want any disunity until after the wedding?'

'It would have upset Mary. Now the wedding's over they'll be told — tonight, in fact. There are bound to be a few nasty moments, my love, but you'll have me to support you, so you've nothing to fear.'

'You're telling them tonight?' She knew that several of the guests were staying at Sandy Creek, having travelled over a hundred and fifty miles or even more in some cases.

'Tonight,' he repeated firmly, and Caryn did not argue; already she knew her husband better than to do so.

'Sharn,' she said after a while, when there had been a companionable little hush between them, 'why did you decide to take us to Alice Springs?'

'I suddenly couldn't bear the idea of your being there with Dick,' he admitted, immediately reminding her that Dick had been showing considerable interest in her.

'He was trying to make Mary jealous,' Caryn put in, and Sharn at once informed her that, after Dick had approached him about Mary, saying he wanted to marry her, he, Sharn, had reached that very conclusion.

'However,' continued Sharn, 'as at the time I didn't know that Dick's object was to make Mary jealous I decided to come along with you to Alice. I must subconsciously have known I cared – or was beginning to care,' he amended, pausing in thought. 'But I expect I wasn't at that time fully aware of any definite feelings of love for you.'

'So you really came because you were jealous of Dick,' reasoned Caryn and added, 'even though, consciously, you didn't realize it?'

'I expect it was like that,' he admitted.

'I believed it was merely to further the affair that was developing between Mary and Greg—' She broke off, aware that she was again voicing irrelevancies. Her husband must have thought so too, because for the next few minutes she was not allowed to speak at all. Eventually, rosy from his ardour and her own turbulent emotions, she was allowed to draw away. Eyeing her in some amusement as she endeavoured to recapture a semblance of calm, he hesitated a moment, then said softly, his lips coming close to her heart,

'We are married, darling. I hope you haven't forgotten? There'll be no need for me to propose, then endure an endless period of waiting before I can own you.'

Her colour fluctuated and a lump in her throat obstructed any words she might have desired to utter in response. It was a moment of sheer unbelievable magic, the soft balmy air around them throbbing with the perfume of roses and wattles and the delicate frangipani tree growing close to where they stood. Away into infinity stretched the plains, away towards the dark outline of purple hills – harsh unrelenting country, terrain of fierce contrasts, but Caryn loved it in all its varying moods. It was now *her* country – her home. She need never leave it; she never could leave it, for here was her heart. She looked up into her husband's face, the radiance of love and joy in her expressive grey eyes. With a swift intake of his breath he caught her to him, caught her to his hard demanding body, and his lips claimed hers in a long and ardent kiss.

She thrilled to his mastery; an exquisite trembling seized her as rapture spread like the flow of warm blood through her veins. Defence was impossible against the dominance of his passion and she lay passive until it had spent itself.

'Beloved,' he murmured, a soft glancing tenderness in his accents despite the unmistakable hoarseness that also edged them, 'let's go home . . . to *our* home . . .'

'We must have been out for ages,' she responded, shyness engulfing her all at once. 'What about the guests?'

'They'll be enjoying themselves. Some might have left, though, and others gone to bed.' He paused a moment as if undecided and then, in some amusement, 'Sandra had been rearranging the sleeping accommodation and she informed me that she had put Mr. and Mrs. Clarke in your room. I was all ready to order her to turn someone else out of their room when I – er – suddenly realized you could do without it anyway.' A pause as she blushed, adorably, and buried her face in his coat. 'You see, darling,' he continued at length, 'I had it all worked out. This, sweetheart, is our honeymoon night, and that's why the family have to be told, immediately, that we're married. Tomorrow we'll fly away to one of the Reef islands, where we too shall have a honeymoon.'

His tender smile found instant response in hers as, with infinite gentleness which seemed totally out of place in one so tough as Sharn, he lifted her face to his.

'Our – our honeymoon night . . .' Sweet ecstasy

swept through her at the thought of sleeping in her husband's arms. How little she had guessed, on staring up at the aeroplane which was taking Mary to the dream island where she was to spend her honeymoon, that she too would soon be plunged into the bliss of giving herself to the man she loved. 'I can't believe it's really happening,' she faltered, her eyes bright with tears.

'Darling,' he chided, but with the tenderest expression in his eyes, 'why are you crying?'

She shook her head, then managed a weak smile.

'It's because I'm so happy . . .' She looked up at him apologetically.

'Silly, absurd . . . adorable child! How pleasant it will be getting to know you.' The words came on a wave of tender emotion, fading to silence as his lips found hers.

Harlequin Plus

A WORD ABOUT THE AUTHOR

For Anne Hampson, writing is more than just a livelihood. It is also an exciting hobby. Time and again she travels to foreign shores, where she mingles with the people who live there, gets to know them and even consigns a few interviews to tape. She takes a great many snapshots, buys dozens of postcards and collects maps of the area. Then, when she returns home to England, she makes notes, files them according to category and begins to write.

But long before Anne became a published author, she led a varied and often challenging existence, gathering a wealth of experiences along the way. Her working life began when she was very young—she left school at fourteen—and she has done everything from running a café to delivering milk at five-thirty in the morning. This last job was arranged so that she could return to school, a teacher-training college, as a "mature" student. And before deciding to write full-time, Anne taught for a number of years.

Anne Hampson likes to describe herself as a collector; not only of maps and picture postcards, but of rocks, fossils, antiques and experiences.

What the press says about Harlequin romance fiction...

"When it comes to romantic novels...
Harlequin is the indisputable king."
—*New York Times*

"'Harlequin [is]...the best and the biggest.'"
—*Associated Press* (quoting Janet Dailey's husband, Bill)

"The most popular reading matter of
American women today."
—*Detroit News*

"...exciting escapism, easy reading, interesting
characters and, always, a happy ending....
They are hard to put down."
—*Transcript-Telegram*, Holyoke (Mass.)

"...a work of art."
—*Globe & Mail*, Toronto